JOHN WAINWRIGHT
THE FOREST

St. Martin's Press
New York

Library of Congress Cataloging in Publication Data

Wainwright, John William, 1921-
    The forest.

    I. Title.
PR6073.A354F6   1984   823'.914   84-11755
ISBN 0-312-29871-4

First published in Great Britain by Macmillion London Ltd.

First U.S. Edition

10 9 8 7 6 5 4 3 2 1

It was the only immediate decision I can ever remember taking. Eric told me and, before the words were out, I'd decided.

I realised, even then, that he should *not* have told me. Working, as he does, in a solicitor's office carries with it certain responsibilities. Confidentiality is one of them. But the firm had been the family's solicitors for years and presumably he thought I already knew. He'd also topped his usual quota of whisky. A little garrulous, I suppose.

'Your father was in, earlier today.'

'Really?'

'Signing his new will.'

'Oh, I see.'

The fact is, I did not 'see'. Up to that point, I was not even curious. Hardly interested. Father must be God's gift to that particular law firm. Buying and selling land and property. Insisting that 'solicitor's letters' must be sent to anybody impertinent enough to cause him even minor annoyance. And, of course, the codicils. To fiddle around with the codicils – to add a little something here or remove a little something there – was almost like a hobby. On average, it happened every six months or so. I recall, a few years ago, the head gardener had produced something rather special in roses. He called it 'Sir Lionel' and it won a few prizes in what were, apparently, important shows. Father was delighted. One more codicil; a gift of a hundred pounds to 'the finest gardener ever to tend my soil'. Less than two years later, that same gardener tripped over a hoe (it may have been a rake, I'm not sure which) and sprawled into the side of the greenhouse, smashing about half a dozen panes. The codicil was cancelled next day. 'Father's will', therefore, was treated as something of a family joke. I still viewed it as such, while Eric continued.

'The whole lot scrapped. Codicils and all.'

'It should, at least, make it shorter and more comprehensible.'

'Quite. Everything goes to Raymond.'

I said, 'Really,' and I pride myself that my voice remained steady and, hopefully, as mildly non-interested as before.

'The whole shooting match.' It was, I think, the whisky talking. Plus, perhaps, a certain amount of 'in the know' bragging. 'The land, the loot, the directorships of the firms, the property, stocks, shares . . . the lot.' He sipped whisky, then added, 'Except, of course, the baronetcy. He can't mess around with that.'

'Fortunately,' I murmured.

I changed the subject. I forget what we talked about for the rest of the evening. Nothing important. The usual trivialities of bar talk. It was early May, 1978 – and no great news around which to spin a prolonged conversation. It matters not. I was in no mood for erudite argument. I had reached a decision. Raymond had to be removed.

A little family history, perhaps. The baronetcy had been earned (some said *bought* and I would not deny that too strongly) in the early nineteenth century. The original Sir Lionel Cutter had built upon the cunning and avarice of his father and grandfather. Coal mining, steel production, shares in a rapidly expanding railway network. Skilful dealing in the stock market. Knowing the right people. Donating to the correct charities. From the point of view of coaxing wealth into making more wealth, he was an expert. The succeeding Cutters inherited the same knack. We were numbered among the top dozen richest families in the United Kingdom. The impression was that we owned half Yorkshire, and not a small portion of Lincolnshire.

And yet only the original baronetcy.

I had my own theories on that score. Basically, they boiled down to the *noblesse oblige* dictum. A selfish, self-centred person commands only contempt. The same can be said of families.

My father was typical. What few friends he had were polite enough to call him an eccentric. In fact, he was the most irresponsible person I'd ever met. *His* comfort – *his* convenience – came first, every time. He had a raving, uncontrollable temper. The temper killed my mother in that, when she was eight months' pregnant, she said some small thing of which he disapproved, he was drunk at the time and knocked her to the ground. I was born prematurely and in giving life to me she died.

Less than a year after her death he re-married, and his second wife gave birth first to a son, Raymond, my half-brother, then a daughter, Elizabeth, my half-sister.

Thus a potted history of the Sir Lionel Cutters, baronets . . . and not a history of which to be proud.

That night then, that night in May, 1978, I left Eric and drove home to the cottage. *My* cottage and *my* home. Originally one of the gamekeepers' cottages, it stood deep in the wood and well away from the main house. I'd lived there almost five years, in preference to living under the same roof as my father. He, too, had been glad to see the back of me. I think my twisted limbs were in some way an affront to his precious 'manhood', and certain it is that his tastes and mine touched at no point. Raymond was his *real* son. A strapping twenty-two-year-old, a hard drinker, something of a general hell-raiser and, I do not doubt, in the opinion of my father a fitting creature to carry the seed of future Cutters in his loins.

I was content enough. I had an allowance; a moderately generous allowance which, I suspect, was some sort of twisted penance for what he'd done to my mother. I'd made the cottage very comfortable, without destroying its original charm. I'd taught myself to cook. Nothing exotic, but well enough to get by. A local woman came in three times a week to clean and polish. I was, in short, my own man with freedom to follow my own likes and hobbies.

All of which would end when father died.

Brothers (and by that I include step-brothers and half-brothers) enjoy or suffer extremes in relationship. Glance through history. Read between the lines. If they love each other, their love knows no bounds; it suffers no qualifications; it is the most pure and perfect love of one man for another. Equally if they hate each other. My loathing for my father was something in the nature of disgust and distaste carried to its ultimate. Similarly, I think, his loathing for me. *Negative* emotions. Had we been other than father and son, we would merely have avoided each other's company and left it at that. But with Raymond it was different. There was a *positiveness* about our mutual hatred. Each had what the other wanted. He had a complete and perfect body. I was the eldest son and would eventually inherit the baronetcy. That was part of it, but the hatred went deeper than that. It was part of the air we breathed. Part of the blood in our veins. In the past – before I'd moved to the cottage – we couldn't tolerate even being in the same room together.

Therefore when Father died (and unless the will was changed) my allowance would most certainly cease, Raymond would be a very wealthy man and *I* would be a baronet – the new Sir Lionel Cutter – without a penny to my name.

Raymond *had* to be removed.

I make no apologies. The title meant nothing; it had been consistently sullied since the day it was granted. But the fortune . . . that was *mine*. The power, the final say-so, the land, the property. So much, and so much good could be done with it. Raymond would waste it. High-life and gambling would see it melt like ice in a furnace. I knew Raymond. Knew his ways. Knew the many lunacies he called 'living'.

Therefore he had to be removed.

Odd. The thought of killing him – the thought of murder – never even crossed my mind. Life was sweet. Sacred. A gift from the gods and something mere humans had no right to

8

destroy. Even the life of a man like Raymond.

I think my own deformity had led me to this firm belief. To live in a twisted frame. To be stared at by strangers. To be in an everlasting state of mild discomfort and nagging pain. It has a certain purifying effect. It teaches the unfortunate to appreciate beauty. Beauty in all things, but especially beauty in a perfectly formed body. Not to destroy that body, regardless of what it contains.

Therefore, a removal, but without a killing.

There was no rush. Father was healthy enough. He'd live at least another dozen years. He was a good horseman, therefore there was little likelihood of his breaking his silly neck when riding with the local hunt. Accidents, of course; but he rarely drove any of his cars. He was not the sort of man to employ a chauffeur and take the wheel himself. Oh yes, he'd live. He might even change his will . . . but that was not something I was prepared to risk.

The weather, that May, was all it should have been. Apart from the occasional hazy period, warm and sunny without being too hot. I wandered the woods which surrounded the cottage. Marvelled, as always, as the new green budded the branches. Saw the arrival of the first birds of summer, watched the native birds busy gathering grass and moss for nests. Watched the grey squirrels, and an occasional red squirrel, flick their way up trunks and along branches. Early one morning, just after dawn, saw a late-home-going badger waddling its way back to its sett. I knew ways through those woods even the gamekeepers didn't know. Secret ways. Short cuts. Gulleys beneath exposed roots, unknown even to poachers. My world, you see. A world of sights and smells I shared with nobody. In past years I watched the hounds and horses race and yell less than two field-lengths away while, at the same time, I stood patiently smiling at the dog fox peeping from his lair. He'd known I was there, but he'd also known I wasn't one of *them*. Those woods were mine. More than a hundred acres of them. Mine! Day or night. Every yard, every inch. I destroyed nothing. I interfered with nothing. I was therefore 'allowed'. Even the rabbits – the stoats, the weasels, everything – started, turned, saw it was me, then continued their play or their work. What I knew, what I saw, I never even told. I shared nothing of those woods with any other human being. My own private world, as remote as the poles from the world beyond those woods. A place to wander. A place to claim. A place in which to hide. A place in which to think.

And oh, those thoughts that May. Thoughts of Raymond and what was necessary.

In retrospect, I think I'd known from the first. Not the details, but the broad outline. The core of my ploy. I knew *what* to do . . . I merely needed time in which to plan how to do it.

It was an old air raid shelter. One of the Anderson shelters of World War II; a small room-sized affair made of thick, corrugated steel with an arched roof. How it had got there in the first place is a mystery. We were, I suppose, within wildly inaccurate bombing distance of Leeds or Bradford, but why position a shelter well inside a wood? As a refuge for gamekeepers or foresters caught in the open, perhaps? That was the only possible answer. I doubt if it had ever been used and I was quite sure it had been forgotten for years.

One thing was absolutely certain. No presently employed estate worker knew of its existence. Father was not the sort of employer to whom men and women devoted their lives. The turnover of employees, both in the house and grounds, was steady and constant. Some only stayed for months. The long-suffering ones stuck it out for a few years. But to my knowledge we employed nobody with more than seven years of service.

It had been positioned at the end of a deep gulley and the wood had long ago taken over possession. The closed steel end backed onto a bank and the sides had been filled in; brambles and hawthorn covered them and the curve of the roof. A birch, past its prime, had been toppled by some long-ago storm and bridged the gulley about two yards from the entrance to the shelter. Ivy and bindweed had, over the years, climbed the branches, formed a curtain and thus a false end to the gully. Like antibodies fighting some foreign matter in the human frame, nature had worked to smother this man-made object which had been positioned in its surround. Tried to claim it, crush it and end its unwanted existence. But the steel had been made to withstand anything short of a direct bomb-blast, and the result was a room – a dungeon – perfectly hidden and known only to myself.

I'd come across it perhaps two years previously. As was my occasional practice, I'd been carefully quartering part of the forest in search of new mysteries. It was late autumn, and the ground had been slippery with damp leaves and grass. The built-up boot of my shorter leg had skidded and I'd tumbled, rolled down the side of the gulley and ended almost at the entrance to the shelter.

Since that day I'd used the shelter as an occasional hide. I'd cleaned out the thick carpet of dead leaves, twigs and soil, tested the bench which ran along one side and found it to be made of good wood and firm enough to hold my weight, and from this most secret of rooms I'd watched for hours as even the most timid creatures of the forest had gone about their business. Its robust build and position made it quite weather-proof. Rain or snow, wind or hail, it was always dry inside the shelter. On a boiling hot day it was shady and cool. The surrounding cover of brush and creepers held back all but the worst of frost. I'd even spent nights there in a sleeping-bag. Even in mid-winter. Watching and listening to a life few other people know exists.

And since finding the shelter I had allowed the forest to mend what small breakage I'd made in my original fall, and formed my own hidden path to my secret room. Along the gulley, where the thickness of years of fallen leaves left no trace, then carefully through the curtain of creepers stitching the branches of the fallen birch.

The perfect prison. The centre-piece of a plan to remove

11

Raymond. All I needed to do was work out the finer details.

'Know thine enemy.' So true! I spent the rest of that May, and into June, examining and discarding various plans. I saw only one side of the situation. Mine. But there was another side, too. Raymond's.

I think I was justified in ignoring his side in that I assumed he knew nothing about the change of will. In the event, a stupid assumption. Father was a braggart. I knew that. I should have guessed he would mention the change to Raymond. They were close. Of a kind. With hindsight, that assumption of confidentiality should never have been made and, in making it, I underestimated my half-brother.

I wanted the fortune . . . not the baronetcy.

He wanted the fortune *and* the baronetcy.

I had also, of course, devalued the baronetcy. Not in my eyes, but in the eyes of my half-brother. It had not been earned. It had not been lived up to. It was a mockery . . . but *not* in the eyes of Raymond.

The truth was brought home to me on the evening of Tuesday, June 13th.

It had been an overcast day, but without rain. Warm, without being sultry. That afternoon I'd walked the footpaths which skirted the fields of the Home Farm. Seeking my usual solitude. Noting, with no small pleasure, that the corn buntings and the finches seemed to be more numerous than in previous years. That the elms spaced along the hedgerows had, so far, escaped the spread of disease. As early evening approached I climbed clumsily over a post-and-rail fence and entered the forest for my homeward journey. I'd met no-one but, over and above the sounds of nature, I'd heard the spluttering growl of a distant tractor, an occasional car horn, and as I neared the cottage the sound of shotguns being fired. More than one gun, and I guessed that one of the gamekeepers and, perhaps Father, were waging war upon what they counted as vermin. What I counted as my friends and neighbours. Jackdaws, perhaps. Crows. Magpies. A rabbit, if one came within range. As always, it sickened me. The magpie; the so-called omen of bad luck . . . but a proud bird, a strutting bird, with black-and-white plumage far beyond any simple beauty within the capability of mere man. And what of the blue-black colouring of the crow? Blue-black . . . but also with a hint of emerald green which was *there*, but when you picked up a fallen feather could never be found. I'd been quietly happy in my walk, but as I approached the cottage and heard the guns, the happiness left me.

I rounded the corner of the cottage, and in the same second saw the twin-barrelled twelve-bore raised, heard the roar of its explosion and threw myself to the left. The shot ripped into my upper arm and right shoulder. There was a moment of numbness, then as I sprawled the numbness turned to an ache and the ache wound itself up to a white-hot pain.

I must have shouted or screamed because I heard running footsteps and the voice of Jem, one of the gamekeepers, shouting, 'Careful, sir. Mr Lionel isn't at home and if he . . .' Then a silence, followed by, 'Oh, my God!'

Then Raymond's slight drawl, 'I was shooting at a wood-pigeon. He stepped directly into my line of fire.'

No wood-pigeon. I know my forest. I know my woods. There had been no wood-pigeon; no flapping, no clatter of wings. Nothing!

The pain prevented me from hearing and remembering whatever passed next. I forced myself to remain silent as Jem carried me, as carefully as he was able without the assistance of my half-brother, into the cottage. Made me as comfortable as he could on the sofa. Bound towels around my arm and shoulder before telephoning for an ambulance.

Then it was hospital, a pleasant unconsciousness and an awakening between cool sheets in a side-ward. I was swathed in bandages across my chest and shoulder and bandages covered my right arm, which was held rigidly at right-angles to my body in an L-shaped steel splint.

The nurse smiled, moistened my dried lips and said, 'And there's a lucky man for you.' Her voice had a soft and soothing Welsh lilt. 'Those old pellets hit just about everything that wasn't going to kill you.'

'The choked barrel,' I muttered, and tried to return the smile.

It made no sense to her, but it made sense to *me*. No woodpigeon. No accident. He'd fired the choked barrel of the twelve-bore in order to keep the pattern of shot tighter. Smaller. More lethal. That instinctive jump to one side had saved my life. A choked barrel at that range . . . I should have had no chest left.

I slept moderately well that night. The after-effects of anaesthetic plus, I suspect, some extra drug they gave me. The next morning I awoke to pain. The medic who visited me tabulated the damage. Smashed collar-bone, smashed shoulder-blade, smashed humerus. Shoulder muscles and upper-arm muscles shredded and ripped from their moorings. A great deal of superficial damage. The bones would mend . . . given time. The muscles wouldn't . . . not completely. Again, given time, I'd be able to move my arm again. Even use it for light tasks. But no more heavy work; the muscles would never again be up to it.

'You're right-handed?' he asked.

'Yes.'

'You'll be able to write letters. Lift a pint of beer to your mouth. That sort of thing. But, if I were you, I'd practise using my left arm more than you have in the past.'

A very honest man, not given to hiding the truth in medical jargon. I thanked him for his honesty and he seemed embarrassed. He need not have been. All my life I'd faced the truth and accepted it. Twisted legs, one shorter than the other. A crooked spine. The addition of a near-useless arm meant little to the overall burden.

I lay with the pain for the rest of that morning and until late afternoon. The Welsh nurse visited me a couple of times, then she went off duty, and a coloured nurse took her place. She, too, was efficient and cheerful. She brought me lemon water to drink. Food – a little food – would begin the next day.

At about four o'clock Elizabeth, my half-sister, visited me. She brought grapes. Black grapes. It amused me a little. Why black grapes? Why should every invalid be brought black grapes? Almost a ritual. You're in hospital, you're out of danger, you are starting the long haul to recovery – *ergo*, black grapes!

Nevertheless, I thanked her and she sat by me.

The talk was desultory and meaningless. The normal, sit-by-an-invalid-and-keep-him-amused sort of stuff. Was I in much pain? Not really. It was bearable. Did I know how long I'd be in hospital? No. Nobody had suggested even an approximate length of time as yet. Did I need anything? Books, perhaps. Biographies, travel books, that sort of thing. In paperback, if possible, then I could leave them for other patients.

'Raymond's in a terrible state. He blames himself. He might have . . .' She couldn't end the sentence.

'Killed me?' I supplied.

'He's in a state of shock. I'm sure he is.'

That I did *not* believe, but made no comment.

'Father suggests a private nursing home.'

'No. I'm fine here.'

'A small portable television set. I'm sure we could . . .'

'No television,' I interrupted. I raised my left arm and motioned to the earphones on the hook above my head and within easy reach. 'I have the radio. Good music, if I choose carefully. And the books, of course.'

'Lionel . . .' She paused and nipped her lower lip between her teeth.

'Yes?'

'I'm sorry.'

'Sorry?' I was at a loss as to what she meant.

15

'You're a little . . . unapproachable.' She coloured slightly as she spoke the last word.

'I – er – I wasn't aware.'

'Hidden away in that cottage.'

'I don't hide,' I said gently. 'I prefer living there.'

'I know, but . . .' Again she stopped before ending the sentence. I waited, and she said, 'Why can't we be friends?'

'I thought we were. Surely, that's why you're here?'

'I mean *real* friends. *Real* sister and brother.'

'We haven't a lot in common,' I said quietly.

'More than I have with Raymond.'

I didn't comment.

'Please,' she said.

'It would be very nice,' I agreed with a smile.

She leaned forward and kissed me on the forehead. It was quite a moment. The first time a woman's lips had touched my skin. It made a difference. A strange difference. For somebody to *want* to be my friend. A young woman, too. Not beautiful, but not plain. A half-sister, therefore nothing carnal. Just friends. *Real* friends.

When she'd left, I pondered upon the episode. Sympathy, perhaps? A member of the family injured and in a hospital bed. A very natural reaction. Much as *I* felt when I saw an injured animal. Not love, but a *form* of love. A sadness. A compassion. A natural tenderness.

And yet, and yet . . .

She was so unlike her true brother. She was in no way brash. She was timid. As timid as a shrew. She was, I knew, terrified of my father. His rages, his oafishness, his normal bull-in-a-china-shop way of life frightened her, and in the past I'd seen her scurry from a room in which he'd been ranting and raging . . . again, much like a startled shrew. Strange. I hadn't known her in the past. Hadn't gone out of my way to know her. Subconsciously, I'd equated her with Father and Raymond. With my step-mother. Not truly of my own kind. And, in taking this mental attitude, I'd done her a disservice. Like me,

16

she was an introvert. Disliked unnecessary noise. Sought peace. Solitude, perhaps.

Oh, yes, it might be nice to have her as a friend.

I fear I made something of a nuisance of myself in that hospital. I was not a run-of-the-mill patient. I refused the bed-pan. I refused to even listen to arguments in its favour. One arm and one shoulder were damaged, but there was nothing wrong with my legs; one was shorter than the other, but I had grown up with that, and to me it was a very natural disadvantage. I could perform my own toiletries. I could walk, and walk I would, albeit a little unsteadily. I was no potty-trained child.

The same with baths. I bathed each day, and I bathed alone. No nurse was allowed to help me undress or sponge me down.

'And what about drying yourself?' demanded the Welsh nurse. 'There's a fine exhibition you'll make of yourself. Trying to towel yourself with one hand.'

'I'll do it,' I assured her.

'You think you're so different, do you?' Her eyes shone with indignation.

'Different?'

'Your body. Man, I've seen too many men's bodies to be shocked any more.'

'Alone,' I insisted. 'It may take a little longer than usual, but I passed the stage of having to be bathed a long time ago.'

Small rebellions, but to me important. I took my pills without complaint. I allowed my dressings to be changed whenever it was necessary. Merely that I claimed the right to be an individual. The right to some degree of privacy. I refused to be one more link in a sausage machine.

Strangely, the medic approved.

'He's injured, not sick. Let him do all he can within reason. He'll learn how to use his left hand more.'

17

I smiled my puny triumph, and the Welsh nurse compressed her lips in mock-disgust.

On the fourth day I was able to sit up in bed. My arm was still held bent and rigid in front of me, but surprisingly I'd already grown used to handling things more or less naturally with my left hand. Elizabeth visited me in the afternoon and brought a small parcel of paperbacks. All biographies and autobiographies, as I'd suggested.

'I went to Leeds,' she explained. 'The selection was much better.'

'Nice of you,' I smiled. 'How much do I owe you?'

'Don't be silly.'

'No. I mustn't let you . . .'

'I thought we were going to be friends.' She blushed slightly as she spoke.

'Of course.' I reached and touched the back of her hand as it rested on the bed. 'I must learn what friendship means . . . and thank you.'

We talked. Easily and with smiles and chuckles. We even teased each other a little. It was a new experience. A very pleasant experience.

'The cottage . . .' I began.

'Don't worry. I've already had a word with the lady who cleans. She'll go in as usual. Have it ready for you when you come home.'

'You think of everything.'

'She was quite pleased.' The timid smile came and went. 'To use her own words, "It will give me time to bottom it".'

'That makes me sound like a pretty filthy individual.'

'No. Untidy.' This time she laughed softly. 'Like all men . . . untidy.'

She didn't colour up any more. Didn't blush. Nor, come to that, was *I* as gauche as I was (still am) with other women. There was true relaxation. A genuine but gentle rapport. Her visit lasted more than two hours and it passed almost as quickly as as many minutes. The thought flickered through my

18

mind . . . to find this new friendship, it had almost been worth being shot at.

As she rose to go, she said, 'Jem asked whether you'd mind him visiting.'

'Of course. Why not?'

'I said I'd ask. I told him I was sure you'd welcome the visit. Tomorrow evening?'

'Fine.' I looked up at her and said, 'And you?'

'In a couple of days. If you don't mind.'

'As often as you can . . . please.'

She smiled, and again kissed me gently on the forehead.

Jem came, but not alone. Raymond was with him.

I ought not to have been surprised. The only regret Raymond had was that he hadn't done what he'd set out to do, but Jem had been there when he'd tried. My half-brother had to know what Jem might say. More importantly, he had to know what questions I might ask, and what answers Jem might give. In my own mind, I had no doubts. It had been an attempt at murder. There was at least a possibility that I might report it as such to the police and, if I did, Jem would be a key witness. Therefore, Raymond had to guard his back very carefully.

Jem said, 'Mr Raymond was kind enough to give me a lift in.'

I grunted make-believe understanding as they settled in chairs alongside the bed.

'The missus sent this.' Jem held out a flat package, carefully wrapped in greaseproof paper. 'Apple pie. Home made.'

I nodded my thanks and he placed it on the bedside table.

Raymond fished in his pocket, then placed a half bottle of whisky alongside the wrapped pie.

'Something a bit stronger. Hide it away from the nurses.'

'I haven't thanked you.' I spoke to Jem. 'You saved my life.'

19

'I just happened to be there, sir.' He looked awkward. Uncomfortable. 'Basic First Aid, that's all.'

'That, too,' I agreed.

Raymond said, 'It was a lousy shot on my part.'

'A near-miss,' I countered. 'But a moving target.'

Jem frowned his discomfort. He was no fool. He knew Raymond and I were saying one thing and meaning another. I didn't want to embarrass him further.

I said, 'Thank your wife for the pie. It was good of her to send it. It was good of you to come.'

'That's all right, sir.' The slight frown left his face 'It's bonny out on the estate these days. You're missing it.'

We talked of the woods and the land. Of the pheasants and the partridges. Of the local poachers and the latest tricks they'd been up to. We talked of Rim and Sal, his two dogs. Cocker spaniels.

'Sal's likely to drop a litter any day now. You fancy one, sir?'

'A dog?'

'Great company when you're walking the forest.'

'A nice bitch,' I decided on the spur of the moment. 'The runt, if she happens to be it. But a bitch. They're more faithful than dogs.'

'Bit of a problem when they're on heat.'

'Sal's no problem.'

'I keep my eye on her,' he grinned.

'I'll do the same,' I promised.

'Agreed then, sir.' He seemed delighted. 'The last bitch out . . . spoken for.'

Thus we talked, Jem and I. About nature, and the things and creatures of nature. My half-brother was not included in the conversation. His world – his life – was far too sophisticated for such simple matters. He pretended interest – pretended to listen – but he said little because he had little to contribute.

After slightly more than half an hour Jem stood up and spoke to Raymond.

He said, 'I'll wait by the car, sir. You'll have things to say to

20

Mr Lionel.'

'Wait *in* the car.' Raymond held out the keys. 'I won't be too long.'

'Thanks.' Jem took the keys, then to me, 'Get well soon, sir. Fresh air's the best medicine of all.'

'Thanks, Jem. And thank your wife for the pie.'

And then we were alone in the side-ward. Just the two of us. The would-be-murderer and the should-have-been-murdered. Not on the face of it, of course. No affection. No love. Neither of us were hypocritical enough for that. But at first a façade of civilised tolerance. An injured man, visited in hospital by a member of his family.

Raymond glanced at the whisky and said, 'I'd get that out of sight before somebody spots it.'

I smiled. A tight, unfriendly smile. I did not feel like playing charades.

'Pity about the pigeon,' I murmured.

'What?'

'The wood-pigeon.'

'Oh, *that*.'

I hated that hint of a supercilious drawl in his voice. The heavily-lipped mouth. The slightly raised eyebrow. The sheer gall of the man to even *be* there.

'You used the choked barrel,' I said softly.

'Did I?'

'I know enough about shotguns. The spread of the shot. It *wasn't* spread . . . not enough to down a wood-pigeon at that range.'

'I must have pulled the wrong trigger.'

'You pulled the trigger you intended to pull.'

'Did I?'

'This little lot.' I touched my bandaged shoulder. 'It was meant for the chest.'

'It was meant for a pigeon,' he said flatly.

'I've been called worse things.'

'Are you suggesting there was no wood-pigeon?'

'Not suggesting. Asserting.'

'In that case, why did I . . .'

'Raymond!' I waved him silent. 'This is a hospital ward. It isn't bugged. Nobody can hear what we say. But we both *know*. That shot was meant for me. Fortunately – for me – I jumped, just in time. Equally fortunately for me Jem was at hand, therefore a second shot was out of the question.' I paused to collect my thoughts. To quieten a slight quaver which had crept into my tone. He waited. Stone-faced. Neither admitting nor denying. Quietly, carefully, I continued, 'You want something *I* have. I want something *you* have. Two things we're unable to share, even if we wanted to. It follows that one of us has to be . . .' I paused for a moment, then said, 'Removed.'

'Die,' he said calmly. 'Be killed.'

'The difference between us. I prefer the word "removed".' I glanced at my splintered arm. 'I look upon my presence here as a warning. Something you did not intend. But that's what it is. I don't play games, but I assume all games have rules. Even *this* game. If I'm wrong, it's unimportant. I'll *make* the rule. The only rule to mean anything. Keep your eyes skinned, little half-brother. Take nothing for granted. That is *your* warning. And the game continues the moment you leave this room.'

'I'll win,' he said softly.

'You'll try,' I agreed. 'But unless you want it to *look* like murder, you'll have to be exceptionally careful. Certain conclusions must, of necessity, be drawn by reason of my being here, in this bed. It's a hurdle of your own making, and *you* will have to deal with it.'

Still softly he said, 'There are ways.'

He turned and, without another word, walked from the side-ward. He closed the door quietly and deliberately behind him. It was an obvious gesture. The 'game' was on!

As I recall the events of that June evening in 1978 I find myself asking certain very obvious questions. Why *did* I warn him? To what purpose? Fair play? That, of course, is ridiculous and no answer at all. It was *not* a 'game'. Even at that time I drew back from the thought of killing him. I was prepared to go to the edge, but not *over* the edge. The difference between us, I suppose. But it was still no 'game'. Therefore, why warn him? Why put him on his guard?

I think, with hindsight, I was trying to scare him off. A gamble that if he *knew* of my awareness that my injuries were the direct result of a deliberate murder attempt, he wouldn't try again. The truth is, I was frightened. At that time I was not a violent man; peace and tranquillity would have satisfied me. If he *could* be scared off – if I *could* dissuade him from another murder attempt – I might sleep easier.

That, at least, was part of it.

In the event it was useless. A waste of time. And as he closed the door when he left, I knew it had been a waste of time.

I left word with the sister that I did not want to see Raymond again; that if he called he had to be refused admission to the side-ward. Not that I expected a second visit from him, but the way I felt it seemed a sensible, even a careful, thing to do.

Jem visited me on two more occasions. Elizabeth came twice – sometimes three times – each week. Father and my step-mother not at all. I was in no way disappointed – indeed, Elizabeth's visits were a great bonus – it was what I'd come to expect. No self-pity, you understand. Merely an acceptance of my own peculiar facts of life. I was (had been as long as I could remember) an embarrassment to the family Cutter. Physically, I was a mild mutation. My taste in music and literature was all wrong. I even found pleasure in poetry. I do not doubt that (Raymond apart) they did not *want* me to die, but nevertheless my death would have brought few tears . . . except, perhaps and I hoped, from Elizabeth.

Meanwhile I progressed steadily towards complete health. I gave the Welsh nurse the half bottle of whisky unopened. I wanted nothing from my half-brother, and as I understood things, hard liquor and drugs didn't mix.

23

'And there's a man with more brains than I gave him credit for.' She eyed the bottle appreciatively. 'A little nip, ocasionally. It makes a nice change from chocolates and flowers.'

The pattern of hospital life moved along its usual slow change. The input of analgesics was lowered and the pain increased slightly, then died. The splint was removed, then the bandages. X-rays showed that the bones were knitting well. Then followed a daily visit to the physiotherapy experts in an attempt to get my shoulder and arm muscles back to as near normal as possible.

It took weeks, and all the time I worked on my plan.

I telephoned my garage and arranged for them to pick up my car, park it inside the hospital grounds and leave the keys with the hall porter. I asked that my family should not be notified of my recovery and release from hospital . . . a request which was met with some puzzlement, but agreed to.

Meanwhile, I worked like the very devil to get strength and mobility back into my right arm and shoulder, while at the same time practising everything (including writing) with my left hand. The result was that by the date of my release from hospital I was almost ambidextrous.

Thursday, July 20th was a sad day. Elizabeth came in the afternoon and we strolled side-by-side along the tarmac paths which criss-crossed the open area behind the hospital. It was glorious July weather and the scent of newly-mown grass perfumed the air. Pied wagtails strutted and see-sawed around the lawns, seeking food among the fresh clippings. Off-duty nurses passed us or sat on the grass soaking up the sun's warmth. It should have been a beautiful day, but it wasn't.

We'd talked of so many other things as we'd strolled. About the books she'd kept bringing me. About an art exhibition which had opened at Lessford and which she'd visited. About so many things. We never seemed at a loss for subjects of mutual interest.

Then after a few moments of pleasant silence, I forced myself to say, 'I – er – I leave here tomorrow.'

'Oh, good.' Her obvious delight almost weakened my resolve. 'Let me know what time and I'll come and collect you.'

'No.'

'It won't be any problem. I haven't . . .'

'No.' My interruption bordered upon the savage. I loathed myself for having to hurt her, but it was necessary. In a quieter tone I continued, 'I'm not coming home. Not immediately. You're the only one who knows. As a favour, don't tell the others.'

'What . . .' She swallowed. 'What are you going to do?' Then hurriedly, 'It's not that I'm being nosey, just that . . .'

'It's all right,' I soothed. I took her hand and squeezed it gently. 'I need to think. Work out my future. Convalesce at the same time.'

'I'm sorry,' she muttered, and the glint of tears sparkled her eyes.

'Why?' This time, I was puzzled.

'I – I didn't know I'd been a nuisance.'

'A . . .' I stared at her. We'd stopped to face each other. 'A *nuisance*? Who on earth . . .'

'You want to be alone. That's what it boils down to.'

'Yes, but . . .'

'I'm – I'm sorry to have imposed myself on you. That's all.'

'Look!' We'd reached a quiet part of the grounds. Nobody could hear. Nobody could see. Not that it would have mattered. I gripped her upper arms and looked directly into her face, and when I spoke my voice had an edge of hoarseness. 'Elizabeth. Believe me, *please* believe me. The only thing I'm sorry about. The only thing I regret. We're half-brother, half-sister . . . that damned relationship. If we weren't . . .'

She'd pulled herself from my grasp and was running down the path towards the car park. She was crying. I couldn't see her face, but I know she was crying. And I stood there knowing I couldn't comfort her. Could never comfort her. I watched her

25

disappear round a bend and my helplessness fed my hatred. As simple as that. As stupid as that. Twisted reasoning. Ridiculous reasoning. It was all Raymond's fault. If he hadn't tried to kill me I wouldn't have landed in hospital; if I hadn't been in hospital Elizabeth wouldn't have visited me; if she hadn't visited me I wouldn't have grown to know her – grown to love her – and be standing here helpless while she ran to her car heartbroken – *ergo all Raymond's fault!*

I left the hospital, mid-morning on Friday, July 21st. I gave a false promise to the medic that I'd visit my own doctor within the next few days, then I collected the keys from the hall porter and walked slowly to my car.

Fortunately, my wallet containing about twenty pounds and my Bank Card had been in the hip pocket of my trousers when Raymond had shot at me. Elizabeth had brought in a new jacket, some clean shirts and underclothes some weeks ago when it had first been decided that I might leave the ward and wander the grounds. I was, therefore, decently dressed.

I drove to the bank, verified my current account, obtained a new cheque book and withdrew a hundred pounds in cash. Then I headed away towards Bordfield and Lessford. Twin cities. More or less of a size. Each sprawling outwards until one touched the other. I could lose myself in the crowds.

I installed myself in a guest house on the outskirts of Bordfield and within easy walking distance of the Lessford boundary. A small place, moderate in everything. Moderately priced, moderately clean and with a moderately comfortable bedroom 'with use of bath'. I booked in for a week, and although the landlady showed mild curiosity about the absence of luggage, the fact that I paid in advance – bed and breakfast – and in cash, assuaged her curiosity.

The next morning I drove to Leeds. Saturday was Market Day and at Leeds Market you can buy most things. I threaded my way between the stalls until I found an establishment which specialised in hardware. The proprietor was most helpful.

'Chain? Yes, sir. How strong?'

'Steel. Stainless steel, if possible.'

'We can fit you up, sir. The best comes a bit expensive, though.'

'Obviously. But I want the best.'

'How much, sir?'

'About four yards.'

'By the metre, sir.'

'All right, four – no, five – metres.'

He brought out the chain. It was about finger-wide.

'Best you can buy, sir,' he assured me. 'Won't rust. Hold a bull-elephant.'

I checked the chain before I bought it. It was strong. Strong enough (more than strong enough) for what I wanted it for. I also bought two first-class padlocks, equally strong but slim enough to thread through the links of the chain.

'Anything else, sir?'

'Something to carry them in, if possible.'

'A nail bag, sir. On the house.'

'I'm obliged.'

The nail bag was perfect. The chain and padlocks could be carried without attracting attention. No rattle. No likelihood of the weight bursting the bottom of the strong canvas. I paid him by cheque. The price of my room had taken too much of my spare cash to do otherwise. He scrawled the number of my Bank Card on the back of the cheque and was satisfied. As I left the stall he was hurrying to deal with a customer who seemed interested in claw hammers.

I dumped my purchase in the boot of the car before I sought my next item. Link-wire. Again as strong as possible and, if possible, coated with something to prevent rust. I found it in a store specialising in gardening equipment. Plastic-covered steel. Just what I needed. The assistant looked slightly surprised when I asked it to be cut into four squares, each

27

twelve inches by twelve inches, but I was the customer and I was paying. Again by cheque.

It was enough for that day. Enough cheques. Enough purchases in one town . . . even one as big as Leeds. I was new to this game and, that being the case, I had to be particularly careful. When what had to be done had *been* done the police would be asking questions. And not just the local police. If I knew Father, everybody from Scotland Yard down would be jerked into frenzied activity.

That word 'removal' kept jumping around in my mind. Not a kill, but a removal. Unlike Raymond I wasn't a killer. I was a removal man . . . but not the sort employed by Pickfords!

I had, you see, taken the first positive step. Until that day it had been merely an idea. A scheme. Perhaps only a dream. But now it was becoming reality. No longer a plan inside my head, but physical nuts and bolts of that plan. The chain, the padlocks, the link-wire. I had no other use for them. Only if I put the plan into practice.

I drove at a very moderate speed back to the guest house. It was necessary; my thoughts were divided between driving the car and the outrage of the criminal act I had in mind.

I contemplated prison. If I was caught I would, most certainly, be sent to prison, and for a long time. The thought of prison frightened me. Cells. Walls. Bars. To be locked away like a caged animal. I loathed zoos, circuses and the like. The animal acts sickened me. Not that I doubted they were coaxed rather than frightened into performing their tricks – the man isn't born who can match a fully-grown big cat fury for fury – but they were never *meant* to jump through hoops, balance on pedestals and the like. They were never *meant* for captivity. Like me, they were free souls and their natural dignity demanded that freedom. Me? My puny, ill-proportioned body could never match their magnificence, nevertheless I claimed some degree of dignity. About the only thing I could claim. But to be restricted behind bars would take even that away and I'd go mad. Nothing surer. Prison would drive me crazy.

For the first time, I toyed with the possibility of danger. With the possibility of failure, and its consequences.

I garaged the car, making sure the boot and its contents were securely locked. Then I had dinner at a decent hotel, returned to the guest house, retired and continued my worrying.

The next day, too.

Since that time I have become convinced that few people, having reached a decision, do not have subsequent doubts. To err is human ... but that glib remark ignores the wild speculations when he who might err contemplates the possible result of such erring. Fate is no respector of persons. 'Murphy's Law' – if a thing *can* go wrong it *will* go wrong – grows at the corner of the mind and tatters the neatly hemmed edges of even the best of plans. H.M. Prisons are over-crowded with men (and women) who at some time 'worked things out', but obviously not with enough care.

That Sunday was a particularly worrying Sunday.

By Monday morning I was feeling better. The prisons were still over-crowded, of course, but if the official statistics were to be believed, fifty per cent of all crime was undetected. The prisons were over-crowded with fools and careless people. I was going to be neither.

First, to the bank for another fifty pounds in cash. Then I started my travels. Steel, angle-iron tent pegs from a camping shop in Bradford. On the Tuesday I tasted sea breeze at Bridlington and bought a short-handled spade; something as near to an army trenching tool as I could get.

On the Wednesday I took a breather. I walked around Bordfield, had lunch, then because rain threatened, took in a film. The worry and tension were building up again, and the result seemed to be that my right shoulder and arm began to ache and stiffen up a little. I was, perhaps, pushing things. I suspected that this was the case. My injuries had mended as much as they were ever likely to mend, but there was still a weakness there. That, plus my mental oscillations, convinced me that I needed a short rest. The film was a complete non-event. So much so, that I forget the name of it. I recall it was a Western; the run-of-the-mill garbage, where the badman wears a black stetson and doesn't shave, and the lawman calls all women – even whores – ma'am, and is obviously going to gun down the badman in the final shoot-out. I slept through most of it, and the sleep seemed to renew my spirits. I found a three-star hotel, enjoyed a good dinner, sipped coffee and brandy in the lounge and felt much better when I set off for the guest house and bed.

On an impulse I drove home the next day. By 'home' I mean the forest. It was neither difficult nor dangerous. I approached from the south west; along cart-tracks rarely used and junctions not sign-posted until I was well beyond the tree-line and in a corner very rarely visited and known intimately only to myself. The car was a Polo. Sturdy enough for rough going and I parked it well out of sight. I took the things I'd bought, packed them all into the nail bag and set off into the trees. It took me almost an hour to reach the Anderson shelter, then I scrambled down the bank and rested with my back to one of the main roots of the birch. I needed the rest and, strangely, it really felt like 'home'. I was immediately at one with what town-people would have mistaken for silence, but it was not silence to me. My ears were instantly attuned to the dozens of tiny sounds. The faint squeak and scurry of a wood mouse. The gentle, hissing snarl of a stoat robbed of its prey. The impatient hoot of a tawny owl disturbed in its rest. The old-fashioned sewing-machine sound of a distant chiffchaff. These and more. Many more.

They were my friends. They sang for me, played for me, amused me and were not afraid of me. They were my family – my *real* family – and as I meant them no harm they, in turn, meant me no harm. They would comfort me rather than try to kill me. They would share what little they had rather than rob me of my entitlement. Why should not St Francis of Assisi have talked and preached his gentle beliefs

30

to such creatures? Why not? They were the only 'people' truly capable of understanding.

I cat-napped until the strength returned to me, then I hid the nail bag and its contents under dead leaves in the farthest, darkest corner of the shelter.

I returned to the car slowly. Cleaned the soil from my shoes with tufts of grass. Took off my coat and brushed the marks of the birch root away, then drove back the way I had come. I stopped at an inn I didn't know for a glass of cider and a Ploughman's Platter. Then I continued back to the guest house.

The trip to the forest unsettled me. The next day (Friday, July 28th) I left the guest house and drove back to my cottage. I hadn't realised how homesick I was. How I missed my own furniture, my own small library, my own hi-fi equipment and selection of records and tapes. It was a beautiful day. Real holiday weather. As if the elements themselves approved of this decision to return home.

Having garaged the car and locked the garage doors, I went into the cottage. It was spotlessly clean. Mrs Buxton had 'fettled it' – to use her own expression – in my absence. There was the scent of furniture polish still hanging in the air. I was home, I was happy, I was near enough well again as made no difference and, above all else, I had my precious privacy.

That night I slept in my own bed with the window open, listening to the voice of the forest. The forest speaking to me. Welcoming me back. Telling me I ought not to have left and that, within its surrounds, I was quite safe.

That weekend, as I strolled the better known tracks of the forest, I met Jem. He wasn't a man given to showing surprise and he greeted me as a friend.

'Mr Lionel. It's good to see you up and about again.'

'Jem.' I nodded pleasant greeting.

He fell in step alongside me and, after walking a few yards, he said, 'She's ready for you.'

'She?'

31

'If you still want her, of course.'

'Oh! The dog.'

'Runt of the litter. That's what you said. She's a bonny little lady. House-trained already.'

'Thanks, Jem.' I smiled my approval. 'Of course I want her.'

'Fine.' He chuckled quietly. A happy man, with a chuckle which was silent, but always ready. 'We'll make our way back to my place. You can pick her up.'

'Fine,' I echoed . . . and something told me this was one of the red-letter days of my life.

She had class. How does class show itself? How does that immediate sign of superiority of its own kind – in man and animal – make itself known? One of the mysteries of creation, I suppose, but there was no doubt. Sal had class. Sal . . . because subconsciously I'd already named her. Sal she was, from the very beginning.

A golden cocker. Only a few weeks old. A chubby ball of light bronze fur, she waddled rather than walked. But she waddled towards *me*. Odd. Wonderful. We recognised each other immediately. Jem picked her up and handed her to me and she struggled to smother my cheek with puppy-licks.

Jem's wife insisted I stay for tea. A real country tea with home-made bread, home-churned butter, home-grown lettuce and tomatoes and a slice of home-boiled ham almost a quarter-of-an-inch thick. The whole topped with a dollop of home-made chutney. The tea hot and sweet and strong. A feast for a king, inexpensive but priceless. I found myself hoping that Father appreciated the true worth of this near-unique couple.

As if in answer to my thought, she said, 'Has Jem told you? We're leaving.' She was re-filling my mug at the time. 'Sir Lionel's given him notice.'

I moved my head and looked questioningly at the gamekeeper.

'His privilege.' Jem fought to keep the bitterness from his tone. 'The poachers have been too busy for his liking.'

'That's ridiculous,' I said angrily.

32

'Oh, they've been around.' He was trying to be fair. Trying hard to see both sides of the coin. 'They caught me napping a couple of times.'

'They catch every gamekeeper napping occasionally.'

'That's what I say.' His wife resumed her seat at the table.

'Stay out of this, missus.' A gentle man, but master in his own house. He was the bread-winner. His was the final responsibility. The gentle censure left no doubt. He continued talking to me. 'It's not as bad as it sounds, Mr Lionel. I think I've got another place. Up near the border.'

'You only think?'

He frowned and added, 'The gaffer won't give me a testimonial.'

'The hell he won't!'

'Sack a man,' he sighed. 'You can't very well say he's much good after that.'

I frowned at my plate for a moment, then said, '*I'll* give you a testimonial. I'll sign it on behalf of my father.'

'That wouldn't be right, sir.' It was a muttered, half-hearted objection.

'Give me the name and address before I go,' I insisted. 'And the telephone number. I'll ring them. Tell them it's on the way. You might as well get in first.'

'I still don't think . . .'

'Jem!'

'Jem.' His wife and I spoke his name at the same time. I said, 'I know these woods better than anybody. Better than you even. Whoever takes over won't be able to keep the poachers down. You've done a damn good job. Don't knock yourself. And don't let anybody – *anybody* – knock you because you haven't done the impossible.'

On the way home I walked slowly. Sal followed me. Puppy though she was, obedience was in her blood. Slow as I walked, her tiny feet fairly twinkled as she ran to keep up with me. She stumbled a couple of times and, as if in protest, she made occasional puppy yaps if I drew ahead. She squatted and emptied her bladder a couple of times then, as I rested on a fallen log, she tried to scramble up my leg and onto my lap. Already neither of us had any doubt as to whose dog she was. I lifted her from the ground and she settled in the bend of my lap. Quiet. Happy. *My* dog . . . for the remainder of her life. I carried her the rest of the way home.

The pettiness of my father. It almost amounted to deliberate cruelty. Gamekeeping was not an over-paid job, and men with land enough to employ gamekeepers tend to value a good man when they get one. Ordinary landowners. Landowners with sense. Not Father. Father was an arrogant fool. As always, he gave nothing and demanded too much. Nor did he give a damn that he was probably throwing a good man into the dole queue; that whoever replaced Jem would probably not be as able and certainly not as loyal.

I brooded on the problem, tried to relieve my mood by putting Ashkenazy's recording of *The Appassionata* on the hi-fi, but to no avail. Like Sal, I was (in effect) the runt of a family; the next Sir Lionel Cutter – assuming I lived long enough – but scorned and without authority. Deformed. Incomplete. Therefore, a mutation in a line proud of its manhood and hard bargaining. I didn't shoot, I didn't ride, I didn't even fish. I drank little and hell-raised not at all. To them – to my father and my half-brother – I was a joke in bad taste. Something to ignore and try to forget.

The hell I was!

I allowed the record to run its magnificently fast coda, then took it from the turntable, placed it carefully into its cover and returned it to the rack. I settled Sal into the comfort of my own armchair, then left the cottage and walked to the house.

Father was in the library. As usual at this time of day he'd been drinking. He wasn't drunk. Not by a long way. The Cutters could hold their liquor! But he was in one of the deep leather chairs, glancing through a copy of *The Field*, with a half tumbler of whisky in one hand and the decanter handy on a small table near his elbow. He looked up as I entered and grunted what I took to be some sort of greeting, then returned his attention to the magazine. I stumped across the carpet and lowered myself into a similar chair to the one he was using.

'Are you very busy?' I asked, with a touch of sarcasm.

'Eh?' He lowered the magazine.

'Busy?' I repeated. 'Could you spare me a moment of your precious time?'

'What the devil!' He dropped the magazine onto the carpet alongside his chair, gulped whisky and glared.

'I don't often come to the house.' I held my temper and sarcasm in check. 'When I do I have a reason.'

'Are you trying to tell me something?'

'Not tell you. Ask you.'

'Money, I suppose.' His lip curled. I was suddenly aware of the likeness of the two mouths. His and Raymond's. The same heavy, sneering lips.

'No, not money.' I took a deep breath to steady my voice. 'A favour.'

'No doubt it'll cost money.'

'It might even save you money in the long run.'

He waited disbelievingly. This man. This greedy fool who because of what he was – of what he'd been born to – had thrown his life away on what he counted as 'pleasure'.

'Don't sack Jem,' I said quietly.

'Who?'

'Jem, the gamekeeper. You've sacked him. Reinstate him.'

'Why the devil should I?'

'He's a good man,' I said simply. 'He works well. Conscientiously.'

'How the hell do you know?'

'I live in the woods, remember. I see the estate workers more than you do. I . . .'

'No!' he growled. 'How the hell do you know he's been sacked? Has he been whining in your ear? Is that it?'

35

'Quite the opposite. He merely mentioned it . . . plus the fact that you might have cause.'

'Too damn true I have cause. Blasted poachers. It's his job to keep them off the land. That's what he's paid for.'

'He does,' I said firmly. 'Not all of them, but there isn't a gamekeeper born who can guarantee that.'

His eyes narrowed as he watched my face. He was searching for the catch. The hidden reason for my visit. Such men always do. To them there always *is* a catch. They measure other people's morals and feelings against their own. To them decency for the sake of decency doesn't make sense. Fine . . . I gave him that extra reason he was looking for.

I said, 'He also saved my life.'

'For what *that's* worth,' he sneered.

'For what that's worth,' I echoed.

'Raymond was there. He could have sent for the ambulance if . . .'

'Raymond was there,' I interrupted grimly. 'And if Jem *hadn't* been there, Raymond would have given me the second barrel.'

It stopped him. Even Father. His beloved Raymond was, I knew, encouraged to enjoy high jinks, but some jinks were a little too high to be tolerated.

'You're mad!' he breathed.

'I'm alive, but only because Jem was there.'

'Damn Jem. What I want to know . . .'

'That's why I'm here,' I said heavily. 'To plead Jem's cause. The rest isn't important.'

'To hell and damnation with Jem!' The explosion was in complete character. 'Tell the stupid bastard he still works for me, if that's what you want. What I'm . . .'

'I'll hold you to that. And thank you.'

I began to push myself upright.

'*Sit down.*'

'Go to hell.'

36

'SIT DOWN!' He almost screamed the words at me, then, when I'd lowered myself back into a sitting position, he snarled, 'You've just called your brother a murderer.'

'Half-brother,' I corrected him.

'Don't split hairs with me, son. You've just . . .'

'He tried to shoot me.' In contrast I kept my tone as matter-of-fact as possible. 'There was no pigeon. There was nothing. Just me. I ducked and the shot went a little wide. That – like it or lump it – in a nutshell. He'll deny it. Of course he will. But *he'll* know he's lying. And he'll know *I* know he's lying.'

He believed me. What else? It was the truth. He fought hard. He didn't want to believe me. It was there in the play of his expression. He really didn't *want* to believe me. But he'd no choice. The truth had been told and he *had* to believe it. But let there be no doubt, he hated believing it and he hated me for making him believe it.

This time he did not try to stop me as I stood up from the chair and left the room. I'd licked him. My father; the most self-opinionated and bloody-minded man I'd ever met. And I'd licked him! As I walked back to the cottage thoughts crossed my mind. For example that I couldn't remember ever standing up to him before. That he'd always frightened me with his hair-trigger temper. That whatever else I was the seed of *his* loins, therefore why *should* I be frightened of him? Why should I ever have *been* frightened of him? Why should I be frightened of *anybody*?

Big thoughts. Revolutionary thoughts. Thoughts which gave me a warm feeling of confidence.

It would be both an exaggeration and wishful thinking to suggest I was a changed man as I walked back to the cottage. Nevertheless, I had a self-assurance which was new to me. I had learned something. That Father was a bully and, like all bullies, there was also a streak of cowardice in him. Stand up to him – refuse to *be* bullied – and he'd fold.

It was a nice evening and still light and, on an impulse, I collected Sal and continued on to Jem's cottage. Jem's wife answered my knock on the door.

'Is Jem in?' I asked.

'He's round the back in the outhouse, seeing to his ferrets.'

I made my way round the cottage. The narrow path ran through grass and nettles knee-high. There, almost completely hidden in the nettles, I saw the man-trap. Rusty. Unused. A relic of the more barbaric days of gamekeeping. I lifted Sal into my arms and paused to stare at it, then I continued to the outhouse, to where I could hear Jem cooing at his ferrets.

He straightened as I entered and slipped the slim, writhing body back into its cage.

'I've talked to Father,' I said. 'You can stay. Forget what he said about sacking you.'

He stared in disbelief.

'He's changed his mind,' I added with a smile.

He closed the door of the cage slowly. Deliberately. He ran his finger-nail across the close-mesh of the chicken-wire.

In a low voice, he said, 'Not under sufferance, Mr Lionel. Don't think I'm not grateful, but not under sufferance.'

It was such an unexpected reaction that I gaped a little.

'Sorry, sir.' He gave a slow, twisted smile. 'Don't think I'm ungrateful, but enough's enough.'

'As bad as that?'

'It'll come again.' We left the outhouse, he locked the door and we strolled back towards the cottage as he talked. 'Tomorrow, next week, next month. He'll sack me again, and there might not be another place going.' Two or three paces of silence. 'You'll still give me that testimonial?'

'Of course.'

'You're a fine man, Mr Lionel, and I thank you.'

'I don't like the idea of losing a good gamekeeper just because of Father's quick temper.'

'I can take quick tempers.' He chuckled softly, as if enjoying a private joke.

'I know. He's bloody impossible!'

'That's not for me to say, sir.'

At the door of his cottage we paused and I said, 'I'll telephone tonight and post the testimonial tomorrow.' There was an awkward pause, then I put Sal on the ground and held out my hand. As we shook hands, I said, 'Good luck.'

'And you, sir. And take care.'

Jem left on August the 10th. It was a Thursday; a high summer day of whorling midges and diving swallows. Sal and I watched them load the van; the men stripped to the waist with sweat running in rivers down their chests and arms. We (Sal and I) stayed at a distance in the cool of the trees. Hidden. Not wanting to say another 'Goodbye'. I was sad to see him go, but at the same time pleased I'd been able to clinch the post he'd wanted. I hoped he'd be happy. That his new employer would value him more than Father. One thing I knew for certain . . . he couldn't value him less!

The van eventually rocked and bounced down the lane and out of sight. Damn the man, I almost envied him. Strong. Virile. All his life he'd have an employer, but he'd never have a master. That was part of his strength, too. He'd never break. He'd never buckle. He wouldn't even bend. We'd been friends. The attraction of opposites. We'd never voiced our friendship; we were of a kind in that respect. But it had always been there.

I'd lost a friend. I wondered if he felt the same.

One more small hatred I could place at Father's feet.

I waited almost thirty minutes then, leaving Sal where we'd been hiding, I went to collect the man-trap.

That summer of 1978 was all a summer should be. A real Beatrix Potter summer; the sort of summer we remember from childhood. Father and his wife spent three weeks touring the French wine country. Raymond travelled to Scotland for a long fishing holiday. Me? I was happy enough. I walked the forest and the fields with Sal. I taught her obedience. Absolute obedience. It wasn't difficult; the desire to please was in the very marrow of her bones. No choke-chains, no smacks, no

39

punishment. She did exactly what I wanted her to do, once she'd worked out what it *was* I wanted her to do. All it required was patience . . . and not too much patience, at that.

We were never apart. When I drove to Lessford for a sack of ready-mixed aggregate, sand and cement she rode beside me. The same when I went for the leg-iron. Where, in God's name, does one buy a leg-iron these days? It was necessary. Vital. I'd rummaged through the junk left in the outhouse at Jem's old place and found an old poker: a steel rod about two-foot long, threaded at one end and with five nuts screwed onto the thread as a makeshift handle. Half-inch thick rod, capable of being bent into a U. Ideal for my purpose. But a leg-iron? I scanned the newspapers for auction sales and, at last, found notification of the sale of 'equipment' from a defunct private zoo up in Cumberland. We went. We waited until the bulk had been sold; until the batches of odds-and-ends were put up for auction. A man – a tinker of some sort – bought a collection of junk, including foot-manacles to keep recalcitrant apes from running wild.

As he dumped the purchase onto his flat cart I approached him.

'Any of this for re-sale?' I asked.

'Depends.'

'I'm looking for a decent bolt,' I lied.

He waved his hand, invitingly.

I found a bolt and held it up.

'Like this,' I said.

'Two quid.'

'Dammit, that's all you paid for the lot.'

'That's when I was buying. Now I'm selling.'

I pretended to hesitate, glanced at the other stuff then lifted one of the foot-manacles.

'Throw this in and you've a deal.'

'Two fifty.'

'Jesus Christ!'

'Take it, or leave it.'

'Two twenty-five,' I bargained.

He held out his hand and I paid him. I made-believe reluctance. He thought he'd driven a hard bargain. He hadn't. I had the last item I wanted . . . dirt cheap at the price.

Time was running out. The sixth sense which comes to men who live hermit-like lives with creatures of the wild warned me. Simple logic warned me. Jem, the only likely witness to that first abortive attempt, was out of the way. Father, and his lunatic hobby of forever changing the terms of his will, couldn't be relied on. That half-brother of mine had to make his move as soon as moderate safety allowed.

On the other hand, I'd blurted out the incident of the murder attempt to Father when I'd visited him about Jem. Very obviously (and knowing Father) that must have popped a cat into the dovecote. I could only imagine the almighty row which must have ensued when Father had met Raymond. But again (and, this time, knowing Raymond) the excuses and explanations would have come thick and fast. Oil on troubled waters. Nothing more certain! Lionel wasn't quite all there. The solitary life he lives. His deformity. What else, but that it must effect his mind? His imagination? What else, but that he must have a persecution complex sky-high and a mile wide?

The checks. The balances. Everything insisted that my time limit was finite.

I started by digging the hole. In the far corner of the shelter and as near the side and end of the shelter as possible. Two foot deep and one foot square, with sides as straight as possible. It was slow work and back-aching work. Twice I hit small boulders which had to be worked loose and, all the way down, I was hampered by roots which had to be either chopped or sawn clear of the heavy soil. For two afternoons I was on my knees, bending forward and reaching down with the trench-tool implement I'd bought. I wore an old boiler suit I used when painting or tinkering with the car, and the sweat poured from me. On the credit side, by reason of my injured shoulder I had

41

become almost ambidextrous, and that was a help. Nevertheless I needed rest when the hole was the depth and size I required.

Two days after I'd finished the hole I began the second stage of my preparations. I needed water, and I wasn't sure how much water. I carried three buckets and a watering-can to the site, then the link-wire, the steel tent pegs were taken from the nail bag and the poker was bent into a Y shape. I mixed the concrete, fed it into the hole, positioned a square of link-wire at intervals as the hole filled and drove tent pegs into the side of the hole immediately above the link-wire. I used a thick twig with which to work the mix into every crevice and release any unwanted air bubbles. I was ultra-careful. As the hole filled I threaded the legs of the bent poker into the mix and held the loop clear of where the surface of the concrete would come with more twigs. I was, I admit, quite pleased with the result. I had no doubts but that it would hold. Hold forever, if necessary . . . but it wasn't going to be forever.

I had water and mix left over. The water I threw into the undergrowth. The mix I used inside the shelter, making a small slab upon which a man might stand, clear of the earth.

And, every minute of the time, Sal stayed with me. She watched; interested but not understanding. I talked to her and she worked hard to understand. The tilt of her head, the prick of her ears, the movement of her tail. Little more than a puppy, but already the communication between us was complete. She learned my moods. Knew when I was happy. When I was downcast. When I was tired. She knew and she responded accordingly. Her natural instinct was to chase wildlife, but in no time at all and merely by the tone of my voice, I taught her that, to be my friend, she must subdue that natural instinct and, above all else, she wanted to please me. A raised finger to the lips quietened her, regardless of how eager she was to give voice. A wave of the hand sent her racing ahead of me, then she'd stop and turn to make sure I was following. Without my encouragement, she never left my side. We ate together and, at

42

night, she slept on an old blanket folded and placed on the foot of my bed.

In return for the joy she gave, I brushed and combed her every day. Kept her clean. Kept her healthy. She had no collar and no lead. She had complete freedom, and not once did she let me down.

At night I'd sprawl in an armchair reading or listening to music on the radio or hi-fi, and she'd be there with her muzzle resting on my slippered foot. As content as I. As happy to be with me as I was to be with her. Our world. We didn't need anybody else. The rest of the world could indulge in wars and rumours of wars. Let them get on with it. Ours was a private world, not given to such stupidity.

Then one evening, shortly after I'd concreted the plug in the shelter floor, we had a visitor.

Sal heard the footsteps first. She raised her head from my foot and rumbled softly at the back of her throat. I put down the book I was reading, dropped my hand and touched the nape of her neck.

'Quiet girl,' I murmured. 'Thanks for warning me.'

The knock on the door was timid. Hesitant.

'Come in,' I called, and prepared myself for whatever might happen when the door opened.

Elizabeth opened the door and stood waiting on the threshold.

'Oh!' The relief, I think, was obvious to see. Then I smiled, rose from the chair and said, 'Please, come in.'

I helped her off with the lightweight mac she'd thrown across her shoulders as a sop to the slight chill of the evening. I waved her to the spare armchair and, as she sat down, she held a hand out to Sal. Sal backed away from the proffered fingers suspiciously.

'Very much a one-man dog,' I explained gently.

'She'll grow into a beautiful creature.'

'She already is.' Then to change the subject. 'Coffee? I was on the point of making myself a cup. Instant, I'm afraid.'

43

'That would be very nice.'

I hobbled into the tiny kitchen. Without the built-up shoe I was very conscious of the difference in the length of my legs. Sal followed me. She could see no deformity . . . she could only see me.

I busied myself making the snack. Two handmade beakers; originally bought for 'special occasions'; this was the first time I'd used them. A matching sugar bowl and milk jug. A plate of assorted biscuits. I placed them on a tray; one of those black, lacquered trays with a Chinese motif. Gaudy dragons and such. Very carefully, I limped back into the living room, moved a pouffe into position between the two armchairs with my foot, and set the tray in place.

Then I returned to my armchair. Sal sat alongside me, and her eyes never left the stranger; the intruder into our world.

As we stirred sugar into our coffees I said, 'It was nice of you to call. We don't get many visitors.'

She leaned forward to take a biscuit – probably in order not to meet my eyes – nodded her head in the direction of the book and said, 'A war story.'

'First World War.' I lifted the book with my free hand. 'Robert Graves. *Goodbye To All That*. It's not a war book . . . an *anti*-war book. A wonderful use of language. I've read it twice, maybe three times, before.'

'You don't believe in war?'

'Who does?'

'It's sometimes necessary, isn't it?'

'Not if diplomats – leaders – those who mould our destiny know their job. Violence. The trump card of the man with a losing hand.'

'Is that why you're a recluse?' she asked hesitantly.

'Because I don't like war?' I almost laughed at her naivety. 'Opting out.'

'You think I – you think *anybody* – can opt out of a nuclear war?'

'In that case, why?'

'What?' I was deliberately dense.

44

'This.' She moved the hand holding the biscuit. 'This seclusion. This cutting yourself off from the rest of the world.'

'I'm alone . . . not lonely,' I fenced.

'It's unnatural.'

'*I'm* unnatural.' And if the words were tinged with harshness I couldn't help it.

'Because you're not an Adonis?'

'Let's say I'm something of an eyesore,' I growled. 'Let's say I'm not gregarious. I prefer my own company.'

'In that case . . .'

'No!' My sudden movement to stop her spilled coffee onto the knees of my trousers, as she made as if to stand up. 'Not you. For God's sake, not *you*. You're – you're different.'

She blushed and relaxed back in the chair. I dusted the wetness from my knees and felt a lout. Sal sensed that something was wrong, looked up at me and moved the stub of her tail, as if to assure me that, whatever the trouble, she was on my side. I suddenly felt empty and monumentally unhappy.

'I'm sorry,' I muttered in a hoarse voice. 'I'm not accustomed to drawing room manners.'

Her face was still flushed, and she seemed to have to force the words when she said, 'I think you try to *make* enemies.'

'No . . . I have difficulty in making friends. That's all.'

'You visited the house.' She tasted the coffee. It was a statement, followed by a pause in which I could insert whatever I felt like saying.

'Father had sacked Jem.'

'And . . . other things.'

'What?'

'You made an accusation.'

'Oh! That?'

She was here. She'd visited me. I wanted her to stay a while. A little small-talk, perhaps. A friendly argument, perhaps. Or if not that, silence while we listened to good music. Anything! Just let her stay a little and not become embroiled with this foul thing which had become part of my life. She was above and beyond such things. Dammit, they didn't concern *her*. It was something between Raymond and myself.

'The house has been like a battleground ever since.'

'I didn't know that,' I muttered.

'Accusing Raymond of murder!'

'Attempted murder,' I corrected softly.

'Father . . .' She closed her mouth, at a loss for words.

'I can imagine what Father said.' My smile was not a pleasant smile. 'I can also imagine what Raymond said.'

'But you don't have to *live* with it. You're out here, away from it all.'

'They ought not to have dragged you into it.' My tone was bitter and accusing. 'It's between Raymond and me. I didn't want . . .'

'You can't go around accusing your brother of trying to murder you. You can't do *that*. What do you expect if . . .'

'But he can go blasting shotguns off in *my* direction? That's allowed, is it? That's not . . .'

'It was an accident. He didn't mean . . .'

'Did you *expect* him to say it wasn't an accident? Did you . . .?'

'Lionel . . . please!' She wasn't far from tears. 'I came here to get away from it all. For a little peace. To – to . . .'

She bit her lower lip and couldn't go on. I felt a louse. We'd had a quarrel. And about what? About Raymond, who else? Rot the man. He was screwing up my whole life. Deliberately. Systematically. He was getting at me any and every way he could.

My cup rattled on its saucer as I fought to control myself.

'I'm sorry,' I mumbled. 'I can't . . .' I took a deep breath. 'You and I. Don't let's *not* be friends. Please.'

She tried to smile, placed her coffee back on the tray and plucked a square of laced linen from her dress sleeve. She touched her nose, gave a tiny sniff, returned the handkerchief to her sleeve and once again tried to smile. This time she succeeded.

'More coffee?' I suggested.

'No, thank you.'

'Music?' I offered.

'Talk,' she said gently. 'That's why I'm here. To talk.'

'What about?'

'About you.' She hesitated, then added, 'About us.'

'Us?' I made it into a small challenge.

'People . . .' She stopped and, woman-like, straightened her dress around her knees, before starting again. 'People – when they're in hospital – there's a certain amount of . . . er . . . emotional atmosphere.'

'Sometimes,' I agreed carefully.

'They – they say things.'

'They say things,' I echoed.

'Things . . .' She swallowed. 'Things they don't mean. Wouldn't say in other circumstances.'

'I wouldn't know.'

'Things they *shouldn't* say.'

'Did it affect you so much?' I asked the question carefully and softly. Like catching a resting butterfly.

She nodded, and lowered her eyes.

Quite deliberately and rather slowly I said, 'I'm not in hospital now. There's no "emotional atmosphere". If you want assurance, I'll repeat what I said.'

'No!' It was almost a whispered whimper. 'You mustn't. You've no right . . .'

'Every man has a right to tell the truth.' And now my voice was low and a little hoarse. 'What I said *was* the truth. Is still the truth.'

'Lionel. It isn't fair. It isn't . . .'

'Of course it isn't fair. Few things in life *are* fair.' I allowed a moment of silence to develop, then continued. 'I love you. Put bluntly, that's what it boils down to. But I'm not *allowed* to love you. Not the way *I* mean. Not the way we both know I mean. But it's happened, as it does happen sometimes, and I'm damned if I see why it should be kept a closely guarded secret. At least not between the two of us.'

47

'Lionel, we can't possibly . . .'

'Of course we can't.' My voice, although still soft, took on a savage quality. 'But we can be honest. I'm no womaniser. I'm no Lothario. The truth? The shape has much to do with it, I suppose, but I'm closing up to a quarter of a century and I'm as much a virgin as I suspect you are.'

'Not because of what you call "the shape",' she breathed. 'It's what's inside that matters. The man. The . . .'

'I'm talking,' I interrupted desperately. 'I'm saying things. Words. The truth, because I daren't *not* tell the truth. I'm talking, because if I didn't talk I might act. And that's forbidden. *Absolutely* forbidden. What other men – normal men – call "love" isn't for me. Not that. Anything but that. Not incest. My God, not incest! But the feeling's there. The emotion's there. As you say . . . it's not fair.' I closed my eyes, took a deep breath, then opened them. In a gentle whisper, I said, 'Just that you know, my love. Just that *you* know. Nothing to fear. Nothing foul. All I want. All I'll ever want. That we have no secrets.'

I remember those words. I remember that stammered speech. As if I'd made it yesterday. As if I'd just ended it. Awkward and muttered. I was a poor substitute for a knight-errant, but at least she knew. She was my lady, and always would be.

I remember her eyes. Shining with held-back tears. Her expression. Infinitely sad . . . but the hold of her head showed a sudden pride beyond my comprehension.

That much I remember. The rest? I think we listened to music. Good music. Brahms, perhaps, or Beethoven. Probably Mozart or Vivaldi. I know we spoke little. Whenever she came, we rarely spoke. That first evening we'd said all we needed to say. All we dared to say. Thereafter, the music spoke for us. Became the link. The forbidden union of which we were both terrified. Terrified, but at the same time proud. Music was our substitute for love-making . . . and it was sufficient.

I kissed her on the forehead as she left. Then and every other time. On the forehead. A gentle touch of the lips on the forehead. I never dared to kiss her on the lips.

In retrospect. That so much love and so much hatred could, at once, occupy the same mind. Sister and brother. Half-sister and half-brother. With equal readiness, to die for one and to kill the other.

No . . . not quite true. Not quite to *kill*. That would have been far easier. Far less complicated. To 'remove' and, in so doing, claim what was rightly mine. Or, if not all of it, enough to last me the rest of my life.

A warped mind inside a warped body? Oh yes, I've heard the argument. I've had the argument thrown at me so many times since those early days. I have even pondered the argument, but never found reason to agree with it. Raymond had to kill me. He desired something which only my death could give him, therefore he *had* to kill me. I, in turn, needed what he would have when Father died or, if not all, enough. And if I didn't take it before Father died, I'd be a pauper. To kill him would have given me it all. The wealth *and* the baronetcy. But I wasn't greedy. The title I would happily have given him, but couldn't while I lived. The wealth he would never part with. I knew him too well. Our mutual loathing left no doubt. We each had motive. Motive, and to spare. He'd tried once with a shotgun, and failed. He'd try again. He couldn't *not* try again.

Therefore . . .

The man-trap was causing me trouble. It was old and solid with rust. It was also, of course, illegal. But so was attempted murder . . . therefore what was one more illegality?

I painted it with turps. Soaked it, then re-soaked it. Then I worked on it with a wire brush and more turps. The hinges of the jaws were locked solid, therefore I squirted penetrating oil onto them until I could get a little movement. The spring worried me a little. Without a good spring the whole contraption would be useless. Without a spring capable of

49

snapping the toothed jaws together before a man had time to jerk his foot clear. And, come to that, hinges which did nothing to hinder the closing of the jaws. For a while – for almost a fortnight – I feared the man-trap would never work. But I was wrong. A steady application of penetrating oil, a regular scrubbing with turpentine applied with a wire brush and then, one day, the jaws closed under the pressure of the spring. That was a day. A day to remember. For the umpteenth time I'd wrestled the jaws open and engaged the pawl attached to the foot-plate. Then I'd stood to one side and applied pressure to the foot-plate with an old walking stick. And the jaws closed with little more than a squeak, and the iron teeth clenched themselves into the wood of the walking stick and gripped. All it needed was more oil and more turps. The long-dead craftsman who'd made that man-trap had made it to last.

Meanwhile, in the gulley and in the shelter, certain finishing touches had to be completed. The concrete had set perfectly. The top of the loop from the bent poker might have been embedded in rock. I linked the loop to the chain with one of the padlocks, then placed the second padlock and the leg-iron within easy reach of the other end of the chain. I carried a camp bed down and a sleeping bag, and installed them along one side of the shelter. I measured, then dug a trench about a yard long and two feet deep just outside and to one side of the shelter. Strangely, it became a matter of personal pride that I forgot nothing. I even provided toilet paper.

Then came the problem of where to position the man-trap.

I gave it some considerable thought. Next time it would not be an 'accident'. Father had been warned. The shindig at the house eliminated *that* particular ploy. *Ergo*, something deliberate. And the most deliberate thing was a make-believe break-in. At night obviously. Something stolen, a certain amount of vandalism . . . and the corpse of the man who'd come downstairs to investigate.

No amount of thought could determine the 'when', but that wasn't too important. On the other hand, I could have considerable say in the 'where'. Raymond was no professional housebreaker and, above all else, he needed stealth. Silence. To awaken me before he was inside might result in yet one more abortive attempt . . . and this time one he couldn't label 'accident'.

I therefore presented him with an open window. The kitchen window at the rear of the cottage. To keep it open seemed reasonable enough, if only to clear the kitchen of cooking smells. Nothing suspicious. Nothing obvious. Just an invitation he couldn't refuse.

Beyond the rear of the cottage – less than twenty yards away – the forest began. No garden. An area of dried leaves and leaf mould. I drove the stake into the ground at a distance which placed the trap directly under the window. Then I scooped out a shallow hollow, wrestled the jaws open, engaged the pawl and positioned the foot-plate in a position where anybody approaching the kitchen window *had* to stand on it. The covering of leaf mould and dried leaves just covered the teeth of the jaws. The trap was set, and I was confident.

Who would be more clever? Who was more cunning?

I knew Raymond . . . therefore I knew the answer.

The note . . .

I toyed with the idea of typing it, but knew that forensic science could identify the machine from which it came. I thought of cutting letters and words from magazines and newspapers but that, too, might be a give-away. I was wise enough to know that I was pitting my wits against a machine. A law-enforcement machine created to out-smart the professionals, much less an amateur like myself.

Eventually, I decided upon capital letters written with my left hand and using a cheap marker pen. I bought the paper and the envelopes at Lessford Woolworths. I bought the marker pen at W.H. Smiths.

I took a sheet of the paper and, wearing gloves, rubbed it clean with surgical spirit. When it was dry, and still wearing gloves, I spelled out the message; left-handed and in capital letters.

NO POLICE.   HALF A MILLION IN USED
NOTES LETS YOU SEE YOUR SON
AGAIN.   DETAILES TO FOLLOW.

I deliberately mis-spelt the word 'details'. A false clue. I'd
need every red herring I could think of. The first two words
'NO POLICE' were, I knew, a forlorn hope. The minute he
read the letter Father would have the place swarming with
policemen. His demands would be impossible to meet, but he'd
make sure they tried.

I counted the 'HALF A MILLION' as a very clever touch.
Invested with enough care, it would provide me with a
moderate income for the rest of my life. When placed alongside
the Cutter fortune it was a mere flea-bite. It also implied that
the person sending the note was not fully aware of the extent of
that fortune. Cunning, you see. Somebody who knew Father
was rich, but couldn't visualise *how* rich.

All in all, I was rather proud of that note.

The envelope I subjected to the same treatment as the
paper. A rub over with surgical spirit, then the address in
left-handed capital letters. Then, still wearing gloves, I
slipped the note into the envelope, moistened the gum with
tap-water – a blood group can be determined by the saliva
used to moisten the flap of an envelope – sealed it, then
slipped the envelope into a small plastic bag and tucked it
away at the back of a dresser drawer.

I then burned everything. The rest of the writing pad, the
other envelopes and the marker. Even the gloves.

All I needed now was a stamp . . . and Raymond.

Since starting this record of what led to my present
predicament, I have been puzzled about one very important
thing. Why kidnapping? I have tried, but cannot put my finger
on the precise moment when the kidnapping of Raymond
became even a possibility, much less a goal to be aimed at. His

52

'removal' . . . yes. Not his death . . . that also. But if not his death, what? Perhaps his 'removal' long enough to make Father *think* he was dead and, thereafter, alter the will. Perhaps that. I think that was at the back of my mind . . . but not kidnapping and certainly not kidnapping for a ransom.

That idea merely grew, very gradually, from . . .

From what?

The Anderson shelter and its potential, perhaps? The sight of the man-trap alongside Jem's cottage? A gradual realisation that it *could* be done? The unspoken knowledge that, short of killing him, or allowing him the opportunity to kill me, I had to disappear somewhere, and yet needed money enough to meet my own meagre needs? Each added its weight. Each reduced the choice. Eventually only kidnapping for ransom remained. A logical end. But when it *became* a logical end – when I recognised it as such – that moment I am unable to determine.

Another thing . . .

On glancing through what I've already written, I notice that I have not mentioned my step-mother. I am not unduly surprised. She is that sort of person. A *non*-person. Lady Grace Cutter. My God! Her personality is zero. She influences nobody, neither for good nor evil. She is Father's bedmate (and not his only one) and she has borne him two children. Her usefulness is finished. She lives at the house, but she is rarely seen. She is Father's wife, but she accompanies him nowhere. She is a nothing, she has served her purpose and now she has been discarded and, from what little I know, seems content enough with what emptiness her life still holds.

And now I've mentioned her. Enough. Her insignificance is such that a mere mention suffices.

Patience was the thing, of course. Patience and, figuratively speaking, never to leave my back exposed. Sal helped in the latter. Each week – almost each day – saw her more obedient. More eager to demonstrate her love for me. I am told by animal experts that a bitch can become positively possessive. Actively jealous of any person or any creature claiming friendship with her master. I have proof of that. Three times during the following weeks her growl warned me of the approach of Jem's replacement. Each time we were strolling in the forest and, each time I'd heard nothing, nor was the new gamekeeper aware of my presence. But the low growl and the rise of the hackles told me, and I had to order her to sit, pending the appearance of the man.

He was a poor substitute for Jem. A born forelock-toucher and not in the same class as a woodsman. The first time we met I had his measure. I heard him stumbling through the undergrowth minutes before we saw each other. I was standing still, Sal was silent and watching, and we spotted him a good thirty seconds before he knew we were there.

'Who the hell are you?' He had the twelve-bore up and the safety catch off even as he asked the startled question.

'Point that gun away,' I snapped.

'I'm asking you a . . .'

'And *I'm* giving *you* an order!' The idiot wasn't fit to carry a gun. 'Lionel Cutter. Son of the man who employs you. Now, point that damn shotgun away, then break it.'

'Oh!' He lowered the gun, engaged the safety catch and opened the breech. He whined, 'I didn't know, sir. I was only doing my job. Poachers, you see. My job's to . . .'

'Shoot poachers?' I mocked.

'Well, no. But . . .'

'You're the new gamekeeper, I take it?'

'Yes, sir.' He touched his cap as he spoke.

'Out to catch poachers?'

'Yes, sir. Sir Lionel was most . . .'

'I can guess.' My lip curled. 'The poachers in these parts aren't the best in the world, but *you* won't catch any of them. I've been listening to you get nearer for God knows how long. I've been *watching* you for all of two minutes.' It was an exaggeration, of course, but the man needed a sharp lesson.

'*Had* I been a poacher – *had* I also been as trigger-happy as you seem to be – there'd be a dead gamekeeper lying around.'

'They – they don't . . .'

'They *do*,' I contradicted. 'They, too, carry guns and if you charge towards them with *your* twelve-bore cocked and ready they won't wait to let you have first shot.'

'Er – yes, sir.'

'A tip. Never point a gun unless you're going to use it . . . and never use it until you know what you're going to hit.'

'Er – yes, sir.' The finger touched the cap again. 'Thank you, sir.'

I left the contemptible man and as I walked away, he called, 'Er – thank you, sir. Thank you.' I have no doubt he was touching the neb of his cap at the same time. Thereafter, and on the two other occasions we met in the woods, I walked past without a word. Without even acknowledging his lickspittle greeting. But each time I knew he (or somebody) was close. Sal gave warning. The back-of-the-throat growl and the rise of the hackles . . . and she was never wrong.

Elizabeth visited me twice, sometimes three times, each week. Sal grew to know her. Not to *like* her (she was the epitome of the one-man dog) but to tolerate her. And those evenings were very special. When we weren't listening to music we were arguing books. Like me, she was an avid reader. I recall the evening we had a long, impassioned argument about Shakespeare.

She stared – almost glared – and said, 'Don't tell me you're one of the "Bacon" believers?'

'No,' I smiled. 'Marlowe. Christopher Marlowe.'

'That's even more ridiculous.'

'Elizabeth, my dear, it is *not* ridiculous. The whole history of the period suggests Marlowe rather than Shakespeare.'

'Prove it,' she challenged. 'Try to convince me.'

'Marlowe was an established playwright.'

'He was murdered by a man called Frizer. Long before any of Shakespeare's plays were written.'

55

'There was an argument,' I agreed. 'Marlowe and three other men – Skeres, Poley and Frizer – were dining together. Tempers were lost. Marlowe tried to kill Frizer, but instead Frizer drove a dagger into Marlowe's eye and killed him . . . supposedly in self-defence.'

'Supposedly?'

'Marlowe,' I continued, 'was a raving homosexual. His lover was Sir Thomas Walsingham . . . a man of some power. Marlowe was also an atheist – had already seen the inside of prison for his atheism – and stood in danger of re-arrest and execution for the Elizabethan offence.'

'I can't see what . . .'

'Wait.' I held up my hand. 'Even accepting the plea of self-defence, the identity of the man Frizer killed has never been fully established. People *said* it was Marlowe. People *still* say it was Marlowe. But there's no record. Now, supposing it was all a put-up job arranged by Walsingham? We're talking about a period of history when such "arrangements" were common enough. Somebody else – not Marlowe – was killed by Frizer. We know for a fact that Frizer was another of Walsingham's lovers. Kill an unknown nobody, claim that the dead man was Marlowe, then smuggle Marlowe to France, to live comfortably and write plays under the name of "Shakespeare".'

'*Shakespeare* wrote them!'

'The first Shakespearian publication was *Venus and Adonis*. It appeared four months after the "murder" of Marlowe.'

'That doesn't *prove* anything.'

'The style is Marlowe's style. Remarkably so.'

'Lionel, dear, you mustn't let your imagination . . .'

'William Shakespeare of Stratford-upon-Avon,' I insisted, 'is recorded as being a small-time businessman and something of an actor. No record of him having been a writer. Illiterate parents. Illiterate children. None of his manuscripts have survived. No original copies of his plays have survived. He made a will, of sorts, but neither the plays nor the manuscripts are mentioned in it. He never strayed far from Stratford, yet he supposedly writes about Venice, about Rome, about a dozen places he knew *nothing* about. The Jews had all been banished from England. Shakespeare never saw a Jew in his life, but one of his most famous characters is a Jew. What could a petty businessman in Stratford know about court life? Nothing! But Marlowe knew ... through Walsingham. Marlowe had travelled to all the locations of the so-called Shakespearian plays. This I grant you.' I held up a finger and smiled at her. 'A fairly common practice at the time. No "pen names", but if a writer wished to remain anonymous he purchased the use of another man's name behind which to hide. Marlowe *had* to remain anonymous. He secretly bought the name of this unknown Stratford nobody ... and began the biggest literary controversy in history.'

She laughed. I think because she had been unused to laughter for so long, she had a strange laugh. A schoolgirl's laugh. Part-laugh, part-giggle. But delightful.

She said, 'You make it sound like an Agatha Christie.'

'It is,' I agreed. 'But I doubt if it will ever be solved. One of three solutions. I plump for the Marlowe ending.'

'Shakespeare for me.'

'We could be both wrong. It could be Bacon.'

Thus the talk. The chatter. A frantic chatter, at times, in an attempt to mask our real feelings. Arguments galore ... but the arguments of a man and woman who, by force of circumstances, *had* to argue – *had* to disagree – if only to keep themselves apart. I loved her for those arguments. Loved her for knowing their purpose. For realising that silence was, to us, a very dangerous state.

Arguments and music. They added up to love. A strange equation. But the only equation we were allowed.

I would have continued that life – indeed I *could* have continued that life – and remained happy enough. Certain things I could not have, but I was content with what I *was* allowed. Peace. Elizabeth. Sal. My forest and all it contained. All else was unimportant. I was at once a dreamer and a realist. I knew the limitations of my chosen world. A twisted frame. A desire for solitude. Also I suppose a hatred, but who can keep a hatred at fever pitch forever? Days passed when I never gave a thought to Raymond. Then, suddenly, it would hit me. Alone in the cottage with Sal. Walking the woods. Like an unexpected slap across the cheek, the realisation would arrive. A man wished to kill me. My half-brother. Somewhere, somehow, he was plotting to murder me. Then for a moment I'd break into a muck sweat. He might do it! He would certainly try. And I'd been foolish enough to forget that fact.

Then I'd leave Sal in the cottage, make my way warily to where the man-trap was waiting, carefully ease away the covering of dead and rotting leaves and squirt oil on the hinges and pawl. With equal care I'd replace the leaf covering, return to the cottage and, for perhaps the next few days, I'd worry that little bit more. Sleep a little less soundly. Stay indoors more than I would have liked.

And for a while those things fuelled my hatred. Like a blacksmith's bellows the heat increased, and for a few days it glowed white hot. The stupidity. The greed. Yes . . . for those short periods of time I think I *could* have committed murder. I wanted so little. Less than my due, in fact. Less than my entitlement. And I was being made to live in fear of death in order to have anything.

Death?

Oh, yes, I feared death. I was no psalm-singing hero. I had no vague visions of a paradise peopled with men and women with complete and beautiful bodies enjoying eternal happiness. My own crooked frame was a minor curse I'd learned to live with. That and the small inconvenience of the pain which was part of my incompleteness. Not agony. Indeed a pain which could be pushed aside and forgotten by good music and good literature. And, of course, by the visits of Elizabeth. But without such distractions it was always there, and I had no wish to suffer it for eternity. I was, therefore, afraid of death.

Life everlasting. *My* life. And, I fear, I was far too much of a coward to embrace atheism. I couldn't even bring myself to be an agnostic. Understand me, I was not a Christian. I said no prayers. But on the other hand I lived with nature, and nature itself was a negation of any 'chemical accident' theory. Therefore I was, in my own way, deeply religious. But it was a very personal religion, compounded of bits and pieces of all the great religions of the world and, as I understood things, one of their common denominators was a continuation of some form of life after what we call 'death'. And if that form of life was in any way comparable to my own life – and forever – the prospect dismayed me. Frightened me. There was no signed and sealed guarantee of peace. No guarantee of happiness. No guarantee of *anything*.

I never showed my feelings. Never spoke of them. Who would understand? Who *could* understand? And yet at times – not often, but sometimes in the small hours when that irritating pain refused to leave me – I wept silently and was terrified.

A routine developed. A strange, catch-me-if-you-can routine. At times I was sure – so damn *sure* – I was being watched by unseen eyes. Raymond's eyes. Sal would growl gently and I'd stop and silence her. Then I'd stand and listen. The knack of tuning out all the sounds that *should* be there, and concentrating the hearing. Listening for the sound that *shouldn't* be there. A form of woodcraft I'd taught myself over the years. Perfected. I'd stand there, motionless for fifteen minutes sometimes. Out-waiting whoever was watching. Listening for the near-inaudible footfall. For the rustle of cloth as he eased a cramped limb. Watching the birds. Noting where they *didn't* land. Where they *daren't* land.

At times, I could almost pinpoint where he was. Couldn't see him. Could never *see* him. But I knew. To within ten yards, I knew where he was hiding. At those moments I tensed my muscles and prepared to dive for cover, while my eyes never left the spot. Like a blind man knowing exactly where the furniture of his home was positioned. That's how well I knew my forest. That's what made me so sure.

In retrospect, I think that is what saved me. That I *was* sure, and that he *knew* I was sure. I think it unnerved him. To him it must have seemed like a form of magic.

At night, just before retiring, I'd let Sal out to perform her final ablutions of the day. I'd stand at the darkened doorway, with the hall light switched off, and I'd follow her with my eyes and ears. She knew why she was out. She wasted no time. Then I'd lock and bolt the door. Check every window . . . except of course the kitchen window. Then (an old trick) loosely rolled balls of newspaper scattered around the downstairs rooms and on the stairs. The rustle as they were stepped upon or as they were accidentally kicked to one side. Enough to alert Sal. And Sal would warn me.

At times I was terrified. At other times I chuckled out loud at the idea of this half-brother of mine thinking he could out-fox me on my own ground.

All through that summer; that full and fat summer of 1978. Even when the days grew shorter, when the night nip returned to the air, the days were glorious. September was more like August, and October saw little change. That October! Specifically, Friday, October 27th. The gold of the day changed to a night of shining silver. A cloudless sky, polka-dotted with stars and a moon which seemed to be newly-minted. I stood for almost half an hour, in pyjamas and dressing-gown, gazing from the bedroom window at a silver-washed landscape which, if only by right of appreciation, was mine. Who else in the whole world 'owned' that place as I owned it? Who else loved it as I did? Pavements, street-lighting, shops, the tatty brashness of so-called 'civilisation' . . . where was the comparison?

I climbed into bed and Sal grumbled, good-naturedly, as my feet disturbed her already comfortable position. I slept – we both slept – until 2.45 a.m. We were awakened by a scream, followed by the sound of a single shot, followed in turn by a string of pain-induced oaths. Sal began to bark the place down, until I silenced her. Then, somewhat gingerly, I opened the bedroom window, looked out and saw that I'd hooked my fish.

I dressed slowly. I was excited. Almost jubilant. I certainly had no regrets. This man – this foul half-brother of mine – had tried to kill me once. Shoot me to death, and make it appear an accident, and merely for the sake of wearing a badge showing an open palm. For the empty privilege of having the word 'Sir' before his name, and the letters 'Bt.' behind it. To kill a man for that! I had no regrets; I dressed slowly and carefully and, through the still open window I heard the swearing and screaming quieten to groans of agony . . . then stop.

I glanced through the window. There was still enough moonlight to see. He'd fainted. This big man – this would-be-killer – had been knocked unconscious by a little thing like pain.

I left Sal in the cottage and, taking a four-battery torch, went outside. I took care as I rounded the corner to the rear of the cottage, but care wasn't necessary. The beam from the torch showed him sprawling and out cold, the jaws of the man-trap biting into his lower leg with all the single-minded ferocity of shark's teeth. There was a revolver about a yard from his outstretched hand. I picked it up, thumbed on the safety catch and sniffed the barrel. The shot I'd heard had come from that weapon. I even recognised it. Father's Smith and Wesson .38; the weapon he'd carried through World War II; the gun he kept, always loaded, in the top right-hand drawer of his desk. 'In case of burglars.' That was his excuse . . . an empty excuse in that it would have taken him at least three minutes to get from his bedroom to the drawer where he kept the gun. But he was legally entitled to own it. Firearm Certificate. Gun Licence. Everything. I think he kept it because he was, as I have already mentioned, a braggart. It made him feel 'manly'. In the past, I'd watched him take it from the drawer and handle it almost lovingly. With put-upon pride. And, in part, to frighten those of us who knew it was loaded. A stupid thing

61

to keep in an unlocked drawer, but not to be wondered at. He was a very stupid man.

I slipped the infernal thing into the pocket of my mac, then turned my attention to Raymond.

He was unconscious, but twitching slightly. I presumed the pain was penetrating the blackness of his mind and reacting on his nervous system. I felt no pity for him. In the first place, he shouldn't have been there, and in the second place the equal and more prolonged pain I'd suffered as a result of his murder attempt had brought no sympathy from *him*.

I checked the jaws of the man-trap. I noted that he was wearing jodhpurs and riding boots and that the steel teeth had bitten hard into the leather about four inches above the ankle. There was a slight flow of blood, therefore at some point they must have penetrated the leather. It seemed possible they might have broken bone, but I thought it unlikely. What did puzzle me were the riding boots. Black and of first-rate leather, polished up to a beautiful shine and with the letters L.C. embossed in gold on the outside of each boot, near the top. They were Father's riding boots. Father's boots? Father's revolver? Unusual but, at that moment and in those circumstances, little more than that.

I nudged him in the ribs with my built-up shoe. Then I kicked him harder. There was no response. He wasn't bluffing. He really *was* unconscious.

I returned to the cottage and brought out a nylon clothes-line. I trussed his hands, after first ripping off the gloves he was wearing. Gloves? Of course. Even amateur burglars – amateur murderers – knew enough to wear gloves. Then I wrestled with the jaws of the man-trap until I was able to drag his leg free of their grip, after which I used more of the nylon cord to fasten his ankles together. There was enough line left to bind him at the knees, to secure his tied hands behind his waist and, finally, to pin his elbows to the sides of his body.

Then came the problem of transportation.

I decided upon a wheelbarrow. It was awkward. The thing tipped twice before I could position him in a more or less safe position. He remained unconscious, otherwise I have little doubt but that he would have yelled at the increased pain. I left the mystified Sal in the cottage and began my journey to the Anderson shelter. It was a slow journey. I had to stop every fifty yards or so. About half-way there I rested. I sat with my back against the bole of a tree and, in the continuing moonlight, stared at this lout who'd come to kill me. The poor, pathetic fool. To kill *me*? Me! And in my own environment? Given the element of complete surprise, and with a twelve-bore shotgun he'd bodged it up. Thereafter what chance had he had? Well, the hard way is the only way some people learn. People like Raymond.

Dawn was not far away when we reached the gulley, and I saw no reason to lower this animal into his hiding place. I merely tipped the wheelbarrow and he rolled, rag-doll slack almost to the entrance to the shelter. I followed him down the bank, dragged him into the Anderson then padlocked the loose end of the chain to his ankle, just below the injury, via the leg-iron. He was safe. Short of pulling his own foot off he would stay there. He might regain consciousness. He might not. Either way he would never make himself heard, and he would never be found.

I trundled the barrow back to the cottage, showered, shaved and, only then, gave further thought to my next move. As I recall, I had egg, bacon and fried tomatoes for breakfast, and I thoroughly enjoyed it. I listened to the early news on the radio, then I went outside, dug up the stake holding the man-trap, then carried the trap into the garage and covered it with sacking before closing and locking the door. A besom brush cleared away all signs of where the man-trap had been and, at the same time, all traces of the activity after the trap had done its work. I collected the gloves and stuffed them into my jacket pocket. Then – and only then – I considered what I should take on my return to the Anderson shelter.

I used a large, zip-topped holdall. First a knife; a woodsman's knife, with an edge like a razor. Then a large roll of
crepe bandage, cotton wool, lint and a bottle of iodine. I then
heated tinned soup; enough to fill a large Thermos jug. The
revolver . . . after some moments of indecision. A screw-
topped bottle of water from the refrigerator. The gloves . . .
they were *his*, so why not? On an impulse – a slight softening
of my resolve – I folded an old army blanket then rammed it
into the holdall before zipping the top closed. It was late
morning before I set out, and I carried the holdall over my left
arm and the besom in my hands. I walked carefully and
slowly, using the besom to eliminate the tracks made by the
wheelbarrow.

Sal was with me. Sal thoroughly enjoyed the stroll. She was
still puppyish and thought the left-right swing of the besom
was some new game. She snapped at the twigs at the end of
each arc as she danced and played ahead of me. That was
fine. Her scuffles helped to destroy the mark of the barrow's
wheel.

And my thoughts? None. Sal was right; that's what it was . . .
a stroll. I felt no elation. I certainly felt no pity. No guilt.
Indeed, quite the opposite. If I felt anything, I felt quite
charitable. A man tries to break into your home, he carries a
revolver and his firm intention is to murder you. What *should*
you feel? Compassion? Sympathy? Regret? Surely not. He had
everything. I had an empty title. Those were the two things in
the twin pans of the balance. Yet, for what little *I* had, he'd
been prepared to kill me.

In this self-argument I was, of course, jumping the gun. We
neither of us yet had these things. But when Father died – and
he couldn't live forever – that's what it would boil down to.

There was also the matter of self-preservation. Nature had
not blessed me with a comfortable or even a particularly
enjoyable life. But it was the only life I had, and I had no
desire to see its end as headlines in the local newspaper.

Therefore, no *real* thoughts. Merely a stroll during which I removed the marks of my previous journey. A romp for Sal. And, from the goodness of my heart, a degree of succour for this foul half-brother of mine.

He'd almost regained consciousness. Sal sat at a distance and watched as I approached him. Cautiously. Ready for any tricks. He watched me – or tried to watch me – through out-of-focus eyes. I had the revolver cocked and ready in my hand.

'Nothing silly, Raymond,' I warned gently. 'I'm not going to kill you, but I won't hesitate if I have to maim you.'

I grabbed him by the legs, just below the knees, and hauled him to nearly the full length of the chain. Then I placed the revolver to one side and out of his reach, unlocked the leg-iron and, with some difficulty replaced it above the ankle of his uninjured leg. The extra pain seemed to bring him to full consciousness and, from behind clenched teeth, he gave an animal-like moan.

I backed away from the shelter and placed the key to the padlock on a ledge in the bole of the fallen birch. Then I took the knife and cut loose the cords. He moved slowly and stiffly and, with each movement, his jaw muscles quivered as he fought to suffer the pain in silence.

Still holding the knife, I said, 'Onto the bench. Take as long as you wish. I want to get that boot off your injured foot.'

It took him almost five minutes. Five very agonising minutes. The veins in his neck stood out as he forced himself to tolerate the pain and, although he made no sound – I do not doubt that he daren't open his mouth without guaranteeing not to scream – his eyes never left my face.

He screamed when I cut the boot lose. It was a sharp knife, but it was also good leather, and the high-pitched keen which was forced from his gaping mouth might have affected a man with any pity in his heart. It did not affect me. I unlaced the bottom of the jodhpurs and rolled the stocking from the foot, then examined the damage. I'd been wrong. The fibula was

65

broken; I could both feel and hear the crepitus as I worked the foot to view the injury. There was also great swelling and discolouration around the torn flesh where the man-trap's teeth had bitten in.

'The bone's gone,' I said calmly, 'and I have no splints. I'll clean it up, put iodine on, then do the best I can with small branches.'

He watched my face, but remained silent.

I have no doubt but that he suffered the agonies of the damned as I used cotton wool and water to clean the wound of blood. As I poured iodine over the injured flesh. As I covered it with lint, then packed it with tight cotton wool. As I bound it firmly with crepe bandage. As I positioned four lengths of branch and fixed them in position with part of the nylon clothes line. He suffered . . . but he was *meant* to suffer.

'Ease yourself into a sitting position,' I ordered. 'But don't move that foot more than necessary. It *might* mend. It certainly won't if you are not very careful.'

I waited until he'd eased himself slowly into a sitting position, with his back to the side of the shelter and his injured leg out in front of him. I unscrewed the plastic cup from the top of the Thermos jug, filled it with water and held it out. He took it a little unsteadily, but drank it all in one gulp.

I re-filled the cup with hot soup and held it out.

He shook his head.

'Take it,' I advised. 'It's all you'll get until tomorrow. If you don't drink it, you'll wish you had.'

He hesitated, then took it and drank it, then a second cupful.

I positioned the sleeping bag on the camp bed, tossed the extra blanket onto the bench, then re-packed the holdall and pocketed the key to the padlock.

Before I left I gave final instructions and advice.

'The camp bed. That's where you sleep. In the sleeping bag. If you need extra warmth, there's the blanket. There,' I pointed, 'that's your toilet. Don't waste time shouting and screaming. Nobody will hear you. Nobody knows about this place. You're here until *I* decide to let you go. When that will be – at the moment I don't know. You'll be fed and watered once a day. Not always at the same time. You'll have time to think. Use it. Remember why you *are* here . . . because *I* want to live.'

I motioned to the patient Sal and we left.

I have told the bare details of what I did, what I said, what I made my half-brother do that late morning of Saturday, October 28th, 1978. No pity, no sympathy but, at the same time, no elation. Like wringing the neck of a chicken, prior to plucking and gutting it for the oven. I hadn't enjoyed it. It had merely been necessary.

And yet, as they stand, they tend to make me appear evil. Taken out of context – forgetting his first murder attempt and why he'd stepped on the man-trap plate – the narrative gives him the dimensions of near-hero. His toleration of pain. The fact that he hadn't spoken a single word throughout. A big man. A hard man.

Perhaps . . . but not a wronged man. The revolver was proof of that.

Therefore, what else?

That first attempt at shooting me would never have brought a conviction in any court. *I* knew that, therefore I didn't complain to the police. Thereafter? To walk into a police station and say, 'My half-brother intends to murder me, can you give me round-the-clock protection?' would have brought a very strange response. I had had to provide my own protection, and had done so. Had he *not* had this great yearning to see me dead he wouldn't have been caught in the man-trap.

Such, indeed, was my reasoning as I walked back to the cottage, the holdall in one hand, the besom in the other. Logical reasoning. Reasoning in no way fanciful.

Nevertheless, I was in a sombre mood – a mood almost of self-disgust – when I reached the cottage. Self-disgust and dirt. I felt in some way dirty. Unclean. As if I'd done a foul and filthy

67

thing. Something disgusting. Me! I could almost smell the stink of filth – invisible filth – rising from my body.

I left the besom by the door, dumped the holdall in the kitchen, closed the kitchen window then went upstairs to have my second bath of the day.

That afternoon I wrapped the man-trap in sacking and stored it in the boot of the Polo. I took the road west and drove hard; out of Yorkshire and into Cumbria. To Kendal, then north along the A6, skirting Lakeland; left at Shap, then left again at Rosgill. A final left turn took me along the eastern bank of Haweswater Reservoir, driving south in the wildest country in England. The road, I knew, ended nowhere; it just stopped at the southern tip of the water. No villages within ten miles. Stark, fell country and in late October (even on a Saturday) a place of utter loneliness.

I parked the car, made my way to the water's edge – to where I knew there was no gentle slope and the water was always deep – and I whirled the sacking-wrapped man-trap and sent it arcing out to where I knew it would never be found.

On my way home I called at the Royal Oak Inn at Appleby for a snack and a drink. I needed both. I also needed the soothing comfort of this six-hundred-year-old coaching inn. Its feeling of everlasting tranquillity. Its silent assurance that today is less than a dust mote just settled on the great mountain of time.

God . . . *what I'd done.*

The sheer magnitude of it came home to me on my way from the reservoir. That I'd stepped well beyond the line of no-return. That if things went wrong – if *anything* went wrong – no excuse would be accepted. Prison. And for a long time. The glass rattled gently against my teeth as I fought the rising panic. The urge to run. The dry-mouthed terror at the realisation of the enormity of my crime.

It was late when I arrived back at the cottage. Very late. I'd driven both carefully and slowly; forcing my concentration upon the driving of the car . . . but only half succeeding.

For the third time that day I bathed.

Poor Sal. She'd been with me on the journey. Her instinct had told her that something was terribly wrong. At times she'd cried quietly, as if trying to share whatever it was I was suffering. She was sad because I was sad. Because she couldn't understand, and couldn't help.

In pyjamas and dressing-gown I sat in my armchair. I drank neat whisky. Slowly – unwillingly – I, like Sal, began to cry, very softly.

The next day was Sunday, and I slept fairly late. It was also with some trepidation that I made my way back to the shelter. The holdall was re-packed; fresh bandages, fresh lint, fresh cotton wool, strips of wood to make a better splint, a Thermos of hot, sweet tea, sandwiches and fruit. I suppose it was an offering. A gesture, if not of friendship then at least proof that I wasn't actually *enjoying* the situation. I was not an evil man. Not even a vindictive man. I'd been jockeyed into this awful exercise. It wasn't of *my* making . . . and, perhaps, above all else, I wanted Raymond to appreciate that fact.

I left Sal at the top of the bank and clambered down into the gulley. Raymond was in the sleeping bag on the camp bed. He was propped up on one elbow and his face was drawn with pain. Pale, too, despite the day's growth of beard. He gave no greeting. Merely watched as I unzipped the holdall and poured hot tea into the plastic top of the Thermos. I carried the tea and the wrapped sandwiches into the shelter, sat on the bench and leaned forward.

'I've brought some fruit,' I said. 'Extra sandwiches, so you'll be . . .'

He brought his right hand and arm up from the far side of the camp bed and the heel of the slashed riding boot smashed me full in the face, the brass spur biting deep into my forehead above my left eye. For the moment I was knocked dizzy, the tea and sandwiches flew from my hand and he had time to deliver another full-blooded swipe, this time to the side of my neck. Then we were fighting, with Sal joining in and gripping the hand wielding the riding boot and, for her loyalty, being banged against the steel side of the shelter.

I threw myself on top of this damned half-brother of mine and that, of itself, was almost enough. Deliberate weight on his broken leg made him gasp with pain. I also found the chain, and enough of it. I flung it round his neck and tightened it with a fury which almost decapitated him.

'Throw the boot outside.' I snarled the words into his reddening face from a distance of less than six inches. 'Throw the boot outside, stop hurting my dog . . . or, so help me, you're dead!' Then to Sal and in a quieter but commanding voice, 'Sal. Leave him Sal. Leave him and sit.'

They both obeyed. One because his life depended on it, the other because her obedience was part of her training.

I pushed myself from him and, staggering a little, left the shelter. I stood with my back to the fallen birch, took out a handkerchief and dabbed the blood from my face. That first blow had almost done the trick. My head pounded and my handkerchief was sodden with red. I gave myself a full two minutes before I spoke and, while I waited, he unwound the chain from his neck. That, too, had done damage; he'd have a swollen neck for some days. *And* Sal had drawn blood.

At last, I wiped the back of my hand across my dry lips and, in as calm a voice as possible, said, 'In case you come up with any other brilliant ideas. I don't carry the keys to the padlocks with me. Destroy me, and you'll merely die of starvation. I feed you, you animal . . . and if not me nobody.' Steadying myself, I stooped, took the fruit from the holdall and tossed it into the shelter. 'That's it for today. That and the sandwiches. You go thirsty until tomorrow.' I dabbed at my bleeding face and continued. 'From now on you'll be on the bench when I arrive. Both hands in view.

70

Anything else like this and I'll break the other leg . . . you'd better believe that.'

I threw the ruined riding boot into the holdall, zipped up the top, then left.

I was in a bad state when I reached the cottage. The front of my face and my head pumped with every heartbeat. Nor was the pain in my neck something to ignore. The bleeding had almost stopped, due to a continued pressure with my handkerchief, but when I sluiced my face with cold water the bleeding started again.

I examined the damage in the bathroom mirror. My nose and around my eyes was already badly swollen and discoloured; I'd end with both eyes blackened. The gash on my forehead was almost two inches long and bone-deep. It needed stitching, but wouldn't *be* stitched. In this sort of situation, doctors were definitely out!

I bathed my face with near-scalding water and, gradually, that eased the pain into a dull ache. Then using lint and strips of plaster I eased the lips of the wound together until there was only a seep of blood. Nevertheless, and whatever I did, the evidence was there. I'd been in a fight and I carried the marks.

Sal, too, was bruised about the ribs. I felt her over with gentle care, was satisfied that no bones had been broken and prayed that there was no internal damage.

'He'll not do it again, Sal,' I promised her. 'Nobody will ever do that to you again.' And she bent her head and licked my exploring hand.

I brewed tea and added brandy. I mixed Sal egg and milk and added her a drop of brandy, too. She was a brave girl. She, too, had taken a beating. Then we settled down, I in my armchair, Sal on my lap, to allow nature to ease away our respective aches and pains.

Elizabeth visited later that afternoon, before it was dark. She fussed a lot when she saw my face but apparently believed my excuse that I'd tripped in the woods and smashed against a fallen log. She was a little cross when I poo-pooed the idea of visiting a medic, but by this time we knew each other well enough not to try to impose one will upon the other's.

Eventually, she settled into her own chair and, to the soft background of Brahms's chamber music, we talked.

'Peace,' she sighed. 'I'm beginning to know why you live out here.'

'Peace?' I pretended not to understand.

'Up at the house.' Again she sighed. 'It's like a three-ringed circus.'

'What now?' I asked. I made it sound as if I wasn't too interested.

'Raymond's gone.'

'Gone?'

'On the tiles, I suspect. His bed hasn't been slept in since Friday.'

'Oh?'

'But his car's still in the garage and Mother fears the worst.'

'What's "the worst"?' I enquired with mild interest.

'An accident.'

'But if his car's still in the garage.'

'Somebody else's car. One of the wild bunch he calls his "friends". She's quite sure he's in some hospital, not knowing where he is or who he is.'

'She has a more vivid imagination than I gave her credit for.'

'Oh, you know her.' She moved a hand in gentle dismissal.

'Actually, I don't,' I said. 'She's not *my* mother.'

'She doesn't often come out of her shell,' she said heavily. 'But when she does it's all very melodramatic. All *Eric, or Little by Little.*'

'Really?'

'And Father's lost his gun.'

'His gun?'

'That gun he wore during the war.'

'Oh, you mean his revolver?'

'*And* his riding boots.'

72

'Probably Raymond borrowed them,' I suggested naughtily.

'Probably so.' She laughed. She thought I was joking. She said, 'You can imagine. It's like a madhouse up there.'

To skate so near the dangerous ice. To tell what amounted to the truth, but turn it into a half-joke. Why? Normally I would not have been interested in either Raymond or Father's riding boots. Neither subject would have deserved passing mention. Probably a 'Really?' – an empty non-question showing a complete lack of interest – but nothing more. Instead, 'Probably Raymond borrowed them.' I wonder. Do criminals usually play tag with the truth? Is it part of the excitement? Part of the God-like feeling of secret superiority?

In effect I was lumping together the disappearance of Raymond, the disappearance of Father's boots and the disappearance of Father's revolver. Playing with fire, because they *were* lumped together.

And a seed was sown . . .

We talked our usual talk. Not empty. Indeed, important to us, but supremely unimportant to other people and, as we talked, the seed germinated. Not conversationally, of course, but tucked away in one of the dark corners of my mind. Silently. Secretly. It germinated, grew and, eventually, flowered. Before she left – before the parting kiss on the forehead – I knew another truth. Such an obvious truth, but one I'd missed until making that near-dangerous remark.

I gave her thirty minutes. Plenty of time to have reached the house. Then, wearing gloves, I took the letter, found a stamp in a cubby-hole of my desk, moistened the stamp with a trickle of tap-water and affixed it to the letter. Then we (Sal and I) drove to Bordfield and I dropped the letter into the box at the main post office.

It was a little like pulling the pin from a hand grenade.

The next day the swelling of my face was at its worst. My eyes were slits in puffed and discoloured flesh through which I squinted with some difficulty. Nevertheless, my captive had to

73

be fed and watered.

I took the Smith and Wesson with me and, when I reached the gulley I stopped, placed the holdall on the ground and cocked the revolver.

'I want to see you,' I called. 'I want to see you on that bench. If I don't see you, you won't eat and you won't drink.'

Beyond the curtain of undergrowth I saw movement. I was in no hurry, and I knew my half-brother must be having some difficulty in moving because of his leg. But in a few moments he was there; sitting on the bench, with his injured leg stretched in front of him and both hands on his lap.

'Stay there,' I warned. 'I have the gun this time. I'll use it, if necessary.'

He nodded his understanding and I left Sal, picked up the holdall and climbed down.

The truth is, he looked a mess. Filthy and unshaven. Hollow-cheeked and tousle-haired. I kept well clear of his reach, squatted by the birch and, still holding the revolver, unzipped the holdall.

'Food or drink first?' I asked.

'Drink.'

It was the first word he'd spoken to me since his second murder attempt had gone wrong.

'Catch.'

I took the Thermos from the holdall and tossed it towards his lap. He caught it, without difficulty, unscrewed the plastic cup-cover and gulped hot tea. I watched, and felt safe enough to uncock the gun.

'Food,' he growled.

'I'll have the flask back first.'

He hesitated, then replaced the top and the cup and tossed the flask in an easy-to-catch throw. I took sandwiches from the holdall and threw the package towards his ready hands.

He ate in silence for some minutes. Savouring the taste, even though it was only cheese. Only when he'd eaten two of the sandwiches did he speak.

'A broken leg,' he sneered. 'Chained up like a dog. And you're *still* terrified of me.'

'Cautious,' I corrected.

'Caution gave you that face.'

'That's *why* I'm cautious.'

'Don't come within reach.' His voice was low and harsh. 'Don't ever come within reach. I'll kill you if you do . . . regardless of how much pain I suffer.'

'If I die,' I reminded him, 'you'll stay here forever.'

He ate another sandwich before he spoke again.

'I'm here forever, whatever happens,' he said at last.

'No.' I shook my head.

'I'll have another drink.' He held out a hand.

'Finish the sandwiches. Then you can have the Thermos back.'

'I want another drink, damn you.' The tone was arrogant and demanding and the hand remained held out.

Very deliberately I said, 'Go to hell. Finish the sandwiches . . . *then* you get a drink.'

'By God, if I could . . .'

'But you can't,' I interrupted. 'You eat when I say you eat. You eat *what* I say you eat. You drink when I say you drink. You drink *what* I say you drink. Get it into that thick skull of yours. You have no choice. No choice at all.'

I had to hold my head back a little, the better to see through the swollen flesh around my eyes. Nevertheless, I watched him like a cat at a mousehole. This one was cunning and utterly ruthless. I was learning. I'd already made one mistake and suffered for it . . . but I was learning.

Softly, but with meaning, I said, 'Father won't like you borrowing his boots. Borrowing his revolver.'

He grunted as he chewed the last of the sandwiches.

'To kill me. Using *his* gun. Leaving footprints from *his* boots. That was the idea, of course.'

'He might not see me again.' He swallowed the last of the sandwiches. 'If he does, *I* won't have to kill you. He'll do it for me.'

'All this talk of killing.' I smiled as best I could, and tossed the Thermos towards his lap. I held myself in readiness. I half-expected the Thermos to come flying back head-high and was ready to dodge. But he was obviously thirsty. He drank the rest of the tea with obvious enjoyment.

As he re-topped the Thermos, he said, 'If you're telling the truth.'

'I'm telling the truth.'

'Let's assume.' He tossed the Thermos gently towards me. 'What sort of condition?'

'I'm sorry?' I frowned non-understanding.

'You don't want me dead.'

'I've already given that assurance. Alive . . . unless I *have* to kill you.'

'Okay. Alive. In what condition?'

I took a Granny Smith from the holdall and threw him an easy catch.

He bit into the fruit, and spoke as he chewed.

'Injured?'

'That's of no real importance.'

'But alive?'

'That final decision rests with you.'

'No.' He munched the apple as he spoke. Calmly. Conversationally.

'I don't know how you broke my leg . . .'

'A man-trap. You trod on it.'

'I don't remember.' He actually chuckled quietly. 'Little man, I could almost admire you. I didn't think you had the guts.'

'I think you were going to say something.'

'The leg.' He took another bite from the apple. 'It's going bad.'

'Bad?' For the moment something close to panic touched me.

'I can feel it. Septicaemia. Given time, gangrene.'

'Have you – have you looked at it?'

76

'I've had broken bones before. I know what sort of pain they give. Not like this.'

'You're bluffing.'

'Okay.' He shrugged. 'I'm asking no favours. Just that you might be interested . . . that's all.'

'I'll . . .' I rubbed my dry lips together. 'I'll think about it.'

Septicaemia. Gangrene. The possibility – the *probability* – haunted me as I returned to the cottage. Even tetanus . . . and he hadn't mentioned that.

Understand me well. I felt no pity for him, but I did not want him dead. I wanted no corpse on my hands. No killing on my conscience. All I wanted was a means of countering that lunatic will of Father's, plus the opportunity to live a normal life span without always having my half-brother plotting my murder. It wasn't much. Great heavens, it wasn't *too* much to ask!

Peace. That's all I asked for. A quiet life and a moderate income. Not to be a millionaire. Not to roar and whore my life away, like Father had done. Like Raymond would do. A share. Not even my rightful share. I wasn't greedy. I wasn't unreasonable. Nothing outrageous. Nothing ostentatious. A quiet cottage somewhere. Near the sea perhaps. A new environment to explore. To keep myself *to* myself. Sal and I. Just the two of us. A new name. A new identity. A few books. Some good music. Solitude. It wasn't an expensive dream, but the dream would turn into a nightmare if it was built upon a corpse!

There was bitterness in my thoughts. That a man entitled to so much should be denied so little. And yet Raymond, who deserved so little . . .

But, my God, he was a hard man.

Reluctantly – contrary to all I'd ever thought of him – I had to give him *that*. If there *was* septicaemia – if there *was* gangrene – his threshold of pain was something to wonder at. A mere passing mention. Nor was he afraid of death. Indeed he expected to die. Accepted the fact that he was not far from a

77

particularly agonising death. But he didn't whine. He didn't plead. Reluctant admiration, mixed with a growing hatred. If necessary, and however great the pain, he'd die with a sneer on his lips and, in so doing, the real victory would be *his*.

With something approaching disgust I threw the holdall into a corner of the kitchen, then went upstairs for a shower. I allowed the hot, needle-spray to play upon my battered face and it seemed to give relief. Relief from the pain and, strangely, relief from my black mood.

The letter arrived at the house the next day. Morning post. By nine o'clock I'd been telephoned and, without giving details, had been told to get to the house as soon as possible. I guessed the reason, therefore I took my time.

We assembled in the library. Father, my step-mother, Elizabeth and myself. My step-mother and Elizabeth were in chairs. My step-mother was weeping quietly. Elizabeth was sitting bolt-upright in one of the hard-backed chairs, her face pale and a mix of fear and worry in her eyes. Father was pacing around like a caged cat, waving the note and blasting off in all directions. He'd already been at the whisky . . . and that didn't help.

'Look at it,' he stormed. He held the letter out for me to read. 'Look at the damn thing. What, in hell's name, do we pay the police *for*?'

'It could be a hoax,' I suggested.

'Don't be such a bloody fool!' He suddenly seemed to notice me for the first time. 'What the devil have you done to your face?'

'I fell, in the forest.'

'Good God!'

'It's not important,' I assured him.

'Of course it's not important.' His voice rose to a shout and he waved the letter. 'At the moment, *this* is the only thing that's important.'

'It says "No police",' I murmured.

'So?'

'Are you going to . . .'

'They're already on their way.'

My step-mother muttered, 'Lionel, you shouldn't have . . .'

'For God's sake, shut up, woman.' The shout wound itself up into a roar. 'The hell I'm going to let some smart-arsed bastard con *me* out of half a million.'

'It might not be a con,' I said mildly.

'All right. It isn't a con. I'm still not parting with half a million . . . just like that.' He strode to the table, poured neat whisky into a glass and drank it in a single gulp. In a slightly quieter voice, he said, 'The damn fool!'

Elizabeth said, 'Father, he could be . . .'

'Don't *you* start. He could be anything. He could be dead. If he isn't dead, I'll get him back without parting with half a million. If he *is* dead, I'll use that half million to trace whoever murdered him.' He dropped the note onto the table and continued, 'But he's still a damn fool. *Allowing* himself to be . . .'

He stopped as we saw the car pass the window and brake to a halt by the main door.

'Just one bloody car,' growled Father.

'And no sirens,' I mocked mildly. 'How disappointing.'

We waited. Expectantly, I suppose. Those two words 'the police' mean different things to different people. To me, at that moment, they meant danger; an organisation against which I had pitted my wits and more than that, an organisation against which it was more than a little foolish to pit one's wits. Therefore, to me 'the police' in effect also meant 'the enemy'. To my step-mother equally 'the enemy', but for a different reason. The note said 'no police' therefore, as far as she was concerned, 'the police' equated with added danger to Raymond . . . therefore 'the enemy'. But to Father? God only knows what he expected. Certainly value for money. Certainly not what he got.

Not merely one car . . . but, also, one policeman.

He entered the library as the maid opened the door and before she could announce him. As lean as a starving wolf and, at first

79

sight, as savage. That first, sweeping, contemptuous glance, in which he seemed to identify and weigh every weakness each of us had made my heart skip a beat.

'Who the hell are you?' blustered Father.

The purred, 'I answer that question when it's asked politely and when I know who's asking it,' set off the tone of the exchange.

'I rang Gilliant . . .'

'Chief Constable Gilliant.'

'I rang Gilliant . . .'

'*Chief Constable Gilliant.*'

The impression was that the conversation had hit a brick wall, pending Father quietening down and acknowledging the full rank and title of the chief of police.

Father took a deep breath, then said, 'I rang Chief Constable Gilliant and demanded action. If this is all . . .'

'If,' drawled the officer, 'by "action" you mean scores of coppers wearing size ten boots, trampling over your flower beds, dropping chewing gum on your carpets, urinating behind your rhododendron bushes. If that's your notion of "action", complete with Fleet Street scribblers and long-distance lenses, I'll be on my way.'

'What!'

'You'll hit the front pages of every national in the country, of course. But if that's what you want . . .'

'Do you know who you're talking to?'

'No.' The officer smiled a contemptuous smile. 'And, be advised. Don't ask me if I care. You might not like the answer.'

'I'm – I'm . . .' Father choked a little as he fought to swallow his wrath. 'I'm Sir Lionel Cutter.'

'Really? Do I bow or curtesy?'

'Who *are* you?' The question came from the back of the throat.

'Rucker.' The sneering smile came and went. 'Detective Chief Superintendent Rucker. Head of C.I.D., Lessford Region. Now, having got the introductions over, do we do it my way or yours?'

'If – if you know what you're doing . . .'

'I know *exactly* what I'm doing. That's why I hold this rank. That's why I'm here. That's why I didn't bring a brass band along with me. Kidnapping . . . or so I'm told.'

My step-mother said, 'Our son, superintendent. We received a letter . . .'

'Yes, ma'am.' Rucker nodded. 'At a guess, with the usual garbage about not telling the police or else . . . I've often wondered why they don't have them printed in bulk. It would be cheaper in the long run.'

'There's the letter,' Father nodded.

Rucker strolled across, read the letter without picking it up. Took a slim ballpoint from his inside pocket and flipped the page over to examine the other side.

'Who's handled it?' he asked.

Father said, 'I have.'

'I have too,' said my step-mother softly.

'You?' He turned his head in my direction.

'No.'

'You?' This time the question was asked of Elizabeth.

'No.' She shook her head.

'The envelope's on my desk,' volunteered Father. 'I handled that, too.'

'Of course you did.' In an odd way, the man couldn't keep the hint of a sneer from his voice. 'So did the postman, so did the sorter, so did the man who emptied the post-box, so did half the employees of the G.P.O.' He left the table and lowered himself into an empty chair, without waiting for the invitation. 'I'd better know who I'm talking to.' Then, to Father, 'You, I take it, are Sir Lionel Cutter.' To step-mother, 'You, ma'am, are Lady Cutter. These other two?'

Father introduced first Elizabeth, then me.

'Who else knows about the kidnapping?'

'Just the four of us.'

'Oh, no.' Rucker's lips curled as he shook his head. 'Your other son, Raymond, knows. The kidnapper – or kidnappers –

81

know. Their wives, fancy women, might know. At this moment, we don't know *who* knows. A tight circle, but not as tight as you seem to think it is. The only certainty is that *they* don't yet know *we* know.'

'Of course we damn-well know.' Father's temper began to show itself again. 'That letter tells us . . .'

'Unless it's the postman, of course,' mocked Rucker.

'Eh?'

'Are you prepared to listen to an expert?' It was a direct challenge.

'Do we have a choice?' Father tried to match him with sarcasm and failed.

'Oh, yes. I can walk out of here and you can consult tealeaves. It won't get your son back, but it won't make a scrap of difference to my salary or my pension.'

'All right.' Father gave a heavy sigh of temporary defeat. 'Your way. You're the strangest copper I've ever come across . . .'

'The *best* copper you've ever come across.'

'. . . but we'll work on the assumption you know your job.'

'Not an assumption. A certainty.' He was, without doubt, the most self-opinionated man I'd ever met. He leaned back in the chair and in a soft, sardonic voice, 'The kidnappers know they *posted* the letter. Beyond that . . . nothing. They don't know it's been delivered. The Post Office being what it is, they can't even be one-hundred-per-cent sure it *will* be delivered. One of the things they have no control over. They'll be nervous. Working on the basis that they're idiots —which they are, anyway, otherwise they wouldn't be getting up to these tricks – they'll be losing sleep. Worrying. Spending a small fortune on newspapers. Watching television news. Listening to the radio news. Sweating bricks that you *may* have told the police.

'Eventually, they'll convince themselves you *haven't* told the police. A false sense of security will set in, and they'll get in touch again. Another letter, perhaps. A telephone call. If it's a letter you'll ignore it. If it's a telephone call, you'll let whoever

82

speaks say as much as possible, then tell him or her it's the wrong number. The object of the exercise is to get them jittery. To panic them into coming into the open a little.'

'They hold the trump card,' said Father. 'They have my son.'

'And can they spend him?' asked Rucker calmly. 'Can they divide him and retire for the rest of their lives on him? No . . . *you* have the trump card. They don't want your son. They want your money. The way *they* think . . . they just *might* get your money, if they can produce your son. All he is is their bargaining counter. And until they're sure *you* know they hold that counter, he's no damn good to them at all.'

'He's my son,' growled Father.

'Dead he's nobody's son.' The cold-blooded logic of this man Rucker was frightening. 'Dead he's nothing . . . not even a bargaining counter.'

'What kind of man are you?' whispered Step-mother. 'Don't you have *any* feelings?'

'Madam.' He sounded annoyed at having to explain what was to him the obvious. 'If emotion could bring him back I've no doubt you could provide enough and to spare. Myself? I don't know him. Why should I be a hypocrite and pretend what I don't feel? My job's to stand those responsible in a Crown Court dock . . . and I'll *do* that.' He paused, then added, 'What I said was meant to be comforting. Dead he's useless. A hindrance. Therefore, they'll keep him alive . . . at the very least until they think they're on firm ground.'

Know your enemy. The phrase repeated itself, like a burden, all the way back to the cottage and until I flopped into the armchair. Know your enemy. I knew *my* enemy – Detective Chief Superintendent Rucker – and he frightened me. Nature seemed to have pared him down to whipcord and bone and, in so doing, to have removed all sympathy and all common politeness. He seemed to sneer at the world; to have an immeasurable contempt for all humanity. It was far more than self-aggrandizement. Indeed, it was the opposite of that. The

83

impression was that his contempt included contempt for himself, merely because he was part of the human race. He was certain of himself in that he considered himself one of the (if not *the*) best detectives alive . . . but, in that, the best of a very unimpressive company.

'One at a time, and in private.'

The remark had brought an angry objection from Father.

'I get nearer the truth, that way.' Rucker had smiled, as if at some secret only he knew.

'Dammit, there's only four of us!'

'Four of you.' The fractional rise of one eyebrow had been a studied insult. 'The nature of the job – policing – demands that nothing be taken for granted. Nothing! Your son has been kidnapped. *Has* he? At the moment, I only have your word for it. That, plus a ridiculous letter which could have been posted by anybody. I need verification . . . some sort of verification. Otherwise? Is it a hoax on his part? Has something else happened to him – something far more serious than kidnapping – and is this a four-sided cover-up? I need a base-line. Something *I* believe. At the moment, the only thing I know for certain is that I haven't kidnapped Raymond Cutter. I start from there. From a truth I know to be a truth. I move forward, question at a time. Person at a time. And, until *I* believe otherwise, every answer is a lie, and every person is a liar. Basic crime detection. You say a crime's been committed. My job is to detect it . . . *my* way.'

It had been an open challenge. A challenge to all of us, but in particular to Father. And after some hesitation Father had nodded, but without grace. I'd been sent back to the cottage to wait.

'I'll be along later. Get your thoughts organised. Get your answers ready.'

And now it was a little like waiting at the door of a torture chamber. I took watered-down whisky, but it made little difference. The stomach churned and I wanted to be physically sick. That's what terror can do to you. Terror and guilt. Inside my head I built towering edifices of possibilities and probabilities. Ghost prisons of what *might* have happened and what *could* have happened.

Raymond? Was he still there at the shelter? Could he, perhaps, have escaped? Made his way back to the house? Was this Rucker's way of making me sweat? Softening me up? Did he already *know*? He was an evil man. Not merely ruthless. Evil! Evil enough to find pleasure in prolonging an agony. Dear God, what *had* happened? What was *going* to happen?

I took Sal for a walk. A short stroll, never more than a hundred yards from the cottage. Rarely beyond sight of the cottage. I let her scamper among the undergrowth, finding new and exciting scents. It pleased me that she was happy, and the pleasure creamed off some of my panic. Nevertheless, I wondered how long he'd be. When would he arrive? What questions would he ask? What sort of a fool would I make of myself? I decided I needed a stiff whisky before the start of the ordeal, and I returned to the cottage. I was too late. He was already there; sprawling in the armchair used by Elizabeth and watching me, with mocking eyes, as my surprise registered itself on my face.

'I – er . . .' I closed the door behind me. 'I've – I've just been taking my dog for a walk.'

He nodded once, but didn't answer. Sal growled her instant dislike of him, and I ordered her to her mat and told her to be silent.

'I – er . . .' I advanced into the room. 'I didn't see you arrive.'

He tilted his head slightly, but still didn't answer.

'I'd have – I'd have been here.'

'Is it so important?' he murmured.

'What?'

'That you should have been here when I arrived?'

'Oh – er – no. I suppose not. Just – y'know – good manners.'

'Good manners didn't prevent me from . . .' the pause was perfectly timed, '. . .making myself at home.'

Oh, God! The holdall was still in the kitchen. What was in it? Damnation, what *was* still in it? For the life of me I couldn't

85

remember.

'Er – tea,' I stammered. 'I was going to brew myself some tea. If – If you'd like . . . Would you care for some?'

'Bribery?'

He was playing with me. He was playing cat-and-mouse games with me. Of course it wasn't bribery. He *knew* it wasn't bribery. It was his way of prodding and teasing. One more minor cruelty in which to indulge.

I was suddenly very angry. A spurt of fury which came and went like a wrongly turned gas jet.

I snapped, 'If a cup of tea is capable of bribing you, you're not the man you claim to be.'

'*Touché.*'

And even that single-word acknowledgement was a vehicle for soft sarcasm.

Tea and buttered crumpets. Shades of Rupert Brooke! It was a form of civilised lunacy, of course. I was at once disgusted and amused; the paper-thin veneer of academic politeness which, for me, covered a fear which made tiny stomach muscles tremble and refused to be quietened. Rucker? He was like a skilled pathologist, enjoying a snack as he performed an autopsy. The scalpels and chisels were there. Razor sharp and wielded by an expert. The manners were there, too. Good table-manners, but behind them the ever-present mockery. The contemptuous eyes. The curling lips. The subtle emphasis on a word here, a phrase there.

'I've questioned the others.'

I nodded.

'They can't add much.'

'Nor can I,' I said in as steady a voice as possible.

'That remains to be seen.' He paused to sip tea. 'When did you see your brother last?'

'When I was in hospital,' I lied. 'He visited me.'

'Hospital?'

'There was an accident with a shot-gun. I was hit in the

shoulder.'

'Dangerous things, shot-guns.'

'Yes.'

'Twelve-bore?'

'Yes.'

'How long ago was this?'

'Oh, some time ago. July time.'

'As long ago as that?'

'*I* live here. *They* live at the house. We don't often meet.'

'Uhu . . . they said.' He bit into a crumpet, chewed, then swallowed. 'Something of an eccentric.'

'I don't mind being called that.'

'No . . . of course not. A gentle madness.'

'What?'

'Eccentricity.'

'Your definition. You're entitled to hold it.'

'They tend to agree.'

'"They"?'

'Your father. Your mother. Your . . .'

'Step-mother.'

'Ah!' He raised the cup to his lips and drank. 'You seem to be accident-prone.'

'What?' The change of subject caught me wrong-footed.

'Shot-guns. Your face. How did you say you injured your face?'

'I fell. Hit a fallen log.'

'Quite a violent fall.'

'Violent enough.'

'Unable to avoid it, I suppose?'

'I may suffer from "gentle madness",' I said coolly, 'but I stop short of self-inflicted injuries.'

'Unable to stop the impact with your hands.'

'Obviously.'

'What do you think of Raymond?'

I stared. He chewed hot, buttered crumpet as he waited for a reply. This zig-zag questioning was something I hadn't been

87

prepared for.

'My – my half-brother?' I stumbled.

He nodded.

'He's been kidnapped.'

'That's not what I asked.' He swallowed. 'What do you think of him?'

'We didn't like each other,' I said bluntly.

'"*Didn't*"?'

'What?'

'You think he's no longer around?'

'I don't know. I – I hope so. Don't – didn't . . . what difference does it make?'

'More than ever *I'm* likely to have.'

'What?'

'Half a million . . . that's the difference.'

We ate in silence for a few moments. I tried to gather my senses; to work out which direction Rucker's questions were leading. I tried to work it out, but couldn't. No direction. That or a convoluted direction which left me completely lost. Probably the latter. He was that sort of man. Had that sort of brain. Normal people couldn't . . .

'Why are you frightened of me?' The sudden question hit my train of thought like a small explosion.

'I – er – I beg your pardon?'

'Scared of me. Why?'

'I'm not frightened of you,' I lied.

'Fear has a stench,' he mused. 'Dogs know that.' He nodded towards Sal. 'Your dog. It knows when somebody, or something, is frightened of it. It knows. *I* know.'

'You, too, can smell it?' I tried to match mockery with mockery.

'Cutter,' he said, softly, 'it's happened too many times for me *not* to know. Too many men have been frightened of me. I don't have to *smell* anything. I watch and I listen. I'm never wrong.'

'Not fear,' I insisted.

'No?' The sardonic eyebrow rose slightly.

'Slight trepidation, perhaps. You're a policeman.'

'And you've done something wrong?'

'No.' I shook my head. 'Just that policemen affect people that way.'

'Why?'

'*Some* policemen. You're one of them.'

'You don't like me?' He reached forward for a second crumpet. 'Don't let it worry you. Very few people do. I'm too good at my job.'

'Enjoy the crumpet,' I mocked softly.

'Thanks. I will.' As he raised his hand to his mouth he said, 'You don't like your father either.'

'I haven't said that.'

'No.' He bit into the crumpet, chewed and, at the same time, said, 'We have that small thing in common. I don't like him either. He tries to be an arrogant bastard.'

'He has his faults,' I admitted.

'Too numerous to mention.' He swallowed, then sipped his tea. 'Why should whoever kidnapped your brother . . .'

'Half-brother.'

'Ah, yes. By all means let's be accurate. Why should whoever kidnapped your *half*-brother steal your father's riding boots?'

'How the devil should I know?'

'But you knew the boots were stolen?'

'Yes.' I watched for the trap.

'You rarely go to the house. Did they mention it this morning?'

'What?'

'Don't play dumb, Cutter. The theft of your father's boots.'

'No. Elizabeth mentioned it.'

'Elizabeth?'

'My half-sister. She visits me fairly frequently.'

'*Really*?' He made the word foul with insinuation.

'Saturday . . . I think,' I said tightly. 'The boots and the gun.'

His cup was on its way to his lips, and he lowered it back onto the saucer and murmured, 'Tell me about the gun.'

'Father's gun.'

'Shot-gun?'

'No.' I wished to God I hadn't mentioned the gun.

'What sort of gun?'

'A revolver. A souvenir from the war.'

'Locked away?'

'No. I'm afraid not,' I sighed.

'Not *loaded*?'

'He has authority to keep it. It's not as if . . .'

'Was it loaded? Was it *usually* loaded?'

'Yes,' I breathed. 'He – he kept it loaded . . . in case of burglars.'

He leaned forward and returned the cup and saucer to the tray. He placed the bitten-into crumpet alongside the cup and in the saucer. He straightened, linked the fingers of his hands behind his neck, tilted his head back and gazed at a corner of the ceiling. All this he did with silent deliberation, and when he spoke it was as if he was voicing his thoughts aloud; gently, scornfully and with an odium of monumental derision.

'This whole damn family is mad. That I accept, because the majority of the human race is, in varying degrees, mad. But there are levels of madness. Levels of lunacy. There are fools who for their own sake – for the general safety of mankind – should never be allowed loose without a keeper. Should be locked away and forgotten. Men who keep loaded firearms lying around the house for anybody to pick up and take away. Madmen. Bedlamites. Dangerous creatures, without an ounce of gumption in what they're pleased to call their brain.

'Your beloved father is one of that type. Guns! Men of low mentality, but great cunning, make fortunes buying and selling firearms. They sell to other men who intend to *use* those firearms. To kill. To maim. To terrify. To make an already squalid world even more squalid. What a waste of time. What a waste of under-the-counter bargaining. What unnecessary wheeling and dealing, with men like your father around.

'Frankly, Cutter, at this moment I don't give a damn about your brother ... your *half*-brother. I've already learned enough to form an opinion. A hell-raiser. A jet-setter. One of the lads of the village. One of the lads the village would be better without. For me, they could keep him – boil him in oil, for all I care – if I only knew where that gun was. An opinion I've already reached. Darling Raymond is where he is because of your father's bragging and his own way of life. Therefore – I repeat – I don't give a damn. But that gun! I would happily let whoever has him *keep* him in exchange for the knowledge of the whereabouts of that gun.'

He paused, then in a slightly softer, but no less disgusted, tone continued, 'You'll never know, will you? *You* won't know. None of your damn family will know. Nobody will know. The next copper who has his head blown off. Has his guts blasted to shreds. The next householder who dies, trying to protect what he's worked for all his life. The next poor sod who's killed trying to make a citizen's arrest. The gun, Cutter, *the gun*. Where did it come from? Where did it originate? Was it merely picked up, loaded and ready?'

He unlinked his fingers, unwound himself from the chair and stood up. A tall man. Thin as a rake, but every gramme controlled and furious scorn. Concentrated, white-hot contempt.

In little more than a whisper, he said, 'I'm going back there. That lunatic father of yours. I don't give a damn if he's a baronet – I don't give a damn if he's a belted earl – tonight he sees the inside of a police cell. I'll be back for statements. You. Your mother. Your step-sister. You'll all stand in a witness box and tell the world about a maniac who kept a loaded revolver in his house ... ready for any thieving bastard to pick up and carry away.'

I never saw Rucker again ... but we'll come to that later.

For the moment I felt I could breathe again. Rucker was

something I hadn't bargained for. Inhumanity, personified. I'd crack. It was something I *knew*. As surely as tomorrow's sunrise, I'd crack during a second session with Rucker.

It was not a pleasing thought. I tried to argue myself out of the conviction, but it was hopeless. Dammit, I *was* guilty. Nor was I a hard-nosed criminal capable of sitting there and defying a police officer. Not that anybody could defy *that* police officer for long!

The gun had been my salvation. A silly thing like that. They'd told him about the riding boots, but hadn't mentioned the revolver. He'd mentioned the boots and, quite naturally, I'd taken it for granted he knew about the revolver. A mistake had saved my bacon . . . for the moment.

I was capable of making mistakes. That realisation did nothing to comfort me either.

I cleared the things away, washed up and toyed with the idea of visiting Raymond. Toyed with the idea, then discarded it. He could miss a day without food or drink. He'd survive. He'd taken the damn revolver in the first place. Basically it was *his* fault. All of it. The homicidal madness he carried around with him . . . all his fault.

And quite suddenly the thought of madness . . .

Rucker had called us a mad family. 'The whole damn family is mad.' His very words. Like a barb on a fish-hook, I could not work that remark free. Even granting that Rucker was the man I thought he was – even granting that he, himself, was part-mad in his atttitude to life – he'd seen more than I'd seen. In his profession he must have seen true madness in all its various forms and degrees.

I stood at the open door of the cottage, while Sal scurried around seeking some spot for her before-bed ablutions. It was a clear October night. A healthy nip in the air. A cloudless sky showing an army of pin-prick stars. A slight breeze which rustled the dry leaves still clinging to the branches of the forest. A night for stock-taking. A night for truth.

Father. A man with an ungovernable rage. A man who counted himself a god among men; who left loaded revolvers lying around in the house; who was a law unto himself; who took pleasure in terrifying those over whom he held authority.

Mad? Some might say so, and I'd be hard put to find decent or convincing arguments.

Raymond. A younger edition of Father. A man to whom murder was the answer to a problem; who wanted everything, and was prepared to kill rather than discuss; to whom human life was as unimportant as a snap of the fingers.

Mad? Certainly he had moments of madness. Equally certainly, he was not normal. Mad, then? At least, not completely sane.

Myself. A twisted body . . . ah, yes, but a twisted *mind*? I was a recluse. Almost a hermit. That, of itself, was not natural. But there was more. I'd taken a fellow-human, chained him like an animal and hidden him in a forest; I'd maimed him and felt no compassion; I fed and watered him, like a beast.

Mad? Oh yes, taken out of context, there was little room for doubt. *I* could justify it, but if my sanity was suspect?

Elizabeth and Step-mother? Those I refused to consider. I thought too much of the former and knew too little of the latter. But the male members of the family. The same blood ran through our veins. The same passions worked on us in different ways. We were 'The Cutters'. We were . . . 'different'. Our solutions to problems were unique unto ourselves.

It was a bad night. Sal grumbled continuously at my restlessness. Suddenly, as if the elements themselves sought to hammer home the truth, a half-gale arose and the rain lashed at the window of the bedroom. I forsook my bed and stood there watching darkness through tiny ripples of water. Hearing the wind, hearing the creak of trees as they fought the gusts, hearing the drum of rain on the glass.

It was midnight – a few minutes after midnight – when I saw the figure, head down and racing for the shelter of the cottage. I didn't know who . . . just that there was great urgency.

I slipped on my dressing-gown, went downstairs, turned on the lights and was opening the door almost at the same time as the hammering.

Elizabeth. Soaked and cold, with a mac thrown over her nightdress. Bare-footed and with her hair saturated and streaming down the front of her face.

'What the . . .'

'Father – father . . .'

'Come inside, you're drenched.'

'Father – father . . .' She stumbled into the cottage and I closed the door. Her breathlessness was such she could hardly speak.

Sal had joined us and was barking the place down.

'Shut up, Sal!' Then to Elizabeth. 'Please. Take your time. Let me get you a blanket. You'll . . .'

'No.' She gulped air into her lungs, then gasped, 'Father's dead. They've just telephoned from the police station.'

A police station – even a superintendent's office – in the small hours. God! The thing I remember most vividly is the stench of old tobacco smoke, being added to by the steady puffing of his pipe by the man whose office we were in. The divisional superintendent. The chief constable. A medic. All in plain clothes, all of whom looked as if they had been dragged from bed and dressed in a hurry. And myself, of course; I must have looked as if I'd dressed in the biggest hurry of all . . . I still wore pyjamas under trousers, jacket and raincoat.

The chief constable was saying, 'There'll be a post mortem and inquest, of course. You'd be well advised . . .'

'Just a minute,' I cut in. I'd been stunned until that moment, but now the realisation arrived with a rush. 'First things first. How did he die?'

'A heart attack.' The medic answered my question. 'The post mortem will verify it. But my money says a heart attack.'

'Where?'

'In the cell.' The superintendent removed his pipe from his mouth long enough to speak.

'Who was with him?'

'Nobody.'

'Rucker?' I snapped accusingly.

The chief constable said, 'Chief Superintendent Rucker went home two hours before your father's death.'

'Who says so?'

'Mr Cutter.' The chief constable used a solemn voice, and what he said had the ring of truth. 'We've already made initial enquiries. *I've* already made initial enquiries. There'll be very detailed statements taken from every person in this building from an hour before your father's death. I can only tell you what I've already learned, and what I believe to be true.

'Detective Chief Superintendent Rucker arrested your father for a serious firearms offence. Your father was placed in a cell, then Mr Rucker went off duty. The officer on cell duty tells me your father was in a very angry mood. He wouldn't quieten down. He was shouting – screaming at the top of his voice – and hammering on the cell door. Twice the officer visited the cell and asked your father to quieten down and go to sleep. It did no good. He seemed to get worse. Then it stopped. Quite suddenly. The cell duty officer went to check and found your father sprawling on the floor. He tried mouth-to-mouth, but it did no good, so he telephoned for a doctor. Your father was dead. We think from a heart attack . . . we'll know for sure after the P.M.'

'Rucker did it.' It was a wild accusation, and I made it mainly because of the o'clock, plus the fact that Rucker frightened me.

'Rucker did no more than his duty.' The chief constable's tone hardened slightly. 'From what I gather, your father considered himself immune from the law relating to firearms.

He wasn't.'

'Rucker's an animal,' I snarled.

'Chief Superintendent Rucker does a good job, his own way. You may not *like* that way. That's your prerogative. But if you've any serious complaints to make, make them officially. Not – as now – in a moment of emotional stress.'

'Rucker was making enquiries into . . .'

'That's enough!' He was the chief constable, and he threw every ounce of rank into the interruption. '*I* know the purpose of his enquiries. So do you. I suggest we keep it like that.' Then in a more normal voice, 'What's happened here, tonight, is not related to those enquiries. Your father's dead . . . and I'm sorry. We'll know *why* he died later on today . . .'

'I want to be there, at that post mortem,' I demanded.

'I see.' The chief constable sighed. 'You're allowed to be, of course but – if in your present mood you're susceptible to advice – I'd suggest you ask your own doctor to attend. The pathologist won't mind, and a fellow medical practitioner will know what to look for, and understand the jargon.'

I nodded my agreement. Gradually, I was getting myself under control.

'We'll need you to – er – identify the body,' said the chief constable. 'Tonight, before you go home, if that's what you want. Or tomorrow after the post mortem. We'll also need you for the inquest.'

'W-where is it?' My foice faltered a little on the question.

'Beechwood Brook Cottage Hospital.'

'In the morgue,' added the medic unnecessarily.

'Tonight,' I gulped.

'Thank you,' murmured the chief constable.

'One more thing,' I said. 'Rucker. I want him taken off the case. The other case.'

The chief constable frowned.

'He's not a nice man,' I insisted. 'He rubs people up the wrong way. Perhaps you're right – it's *his* way – but we've trouble enough . . . surely?'

'You've trouble enough.' The chief constable gave a quick, tight smile. 'I'll take him off the case. Meanwhile, we'll take you to the hospital, then a short statement of identification and we'll let you know the time of the inquest.'

It was almost dawn as I drove home. Slowly. Pensively. The delayed shock had produced an odd feeling; the sort of not-quite-of-this-world feeling which immediately follows serious illness. The heater of the Polo functioned well enough but, because of my dress, because of the shock, because of the pre-dawn chill, I felt cold and miserable.

Father. There, on the stainless steel slab of the hospital mortuary. They'd stripped him ready for the pathologist's knife, then covered him with a sheet. They'd pulled the sheet away from his face, almost to chest level and for the moment – for that first moment – I hadn't recognised him. Dead. There is nothing looks more *dead* than a human corpse. All that crap about 'looking as if he's asleep'. Hogwash! *They look dead.* Souls, perhaps? Souls leaving the body? I wouldn't know. Just that the difference is the difference between a living tree and a plank of wood. The components are the same . . . *but.*

That 'but'. The most final 'but' in the world.

The rain had eased to a steady drizzle. The wind had dropped. As if the world was in mourning at the death of Sir Lionel Cutter. The thought flashed through my mind then, after the thought, the realisation.

I was now Sir Lionel Cutter.

Good God! A baronet . . . and a pauper.

And from that thought, another realisation. Raymond. Raymond had to be told. He had to be visited; fed and watered; his leg re-dressed and cleaned up. The 'kidnap' scheme was still viable. Still necessary. It had already gone too far. It *had* to succeed, and the fact of my father's unexpected death made not a scrap of difference.

97

Back at the cottage I took a hot shower, changed into dry clothing and packed the holdall. Nobody at the house knew I was back and I wanted to keep it that way until I'd visited Raymond. I dressed for the weather and, with Sal accompanying me, set off for the shelter and Raymond. My cursed foot prevented me from travelling at more than a stumbling hurry, but I made good time.

When I called to him from the shelter of the birch he at first made no answer. He was still in bed . . . presumably asleep. But when he did reply he was in a bad mood.

'Where the hell have you . . .'

'That's enough!' I stepped into view with the Smith and Wessen pointed and cocked. There was a rasping quality to my voice as I said, 'Little brother, don't push me. Take my word for it, since you saw me last I've had *enough*. A tiny pressure on this forefinger and at least one of my problems goes away.'

I watched, as he climbed awkwardly from the sleeping bag, then sat on the edge of the camp bed.

Without undue emotion I said, 'Father's dead.'

He stared.

'Appropriately enough at a police station,' I added.

'How – how . . .'

'His heart gave out. He lost his temper once too often.'

'Good God!'

'It can be argued,' I mused, 'that *you* killed him. You stole this thing.' I moved the revolver. 'A man called Rucker – a detective – learned about it. Learned about his habit of leaving it lying around, loaded and ready. Learned that it had been stolen . . . by you. He arrested Father, Father wasn't amused and his heart couldn't stand the strain. That in a nutshell. Killing people – attempting to kill people – you have quite a flair.'

'Who told them I took it?' he muttered.

'Nobody. Just that it was there to be taken, and that somebody took it.'

For a moment he looked sad, and I don't think it was play-acting.

98

As if trying to fully convince himself, he murmured, 'For all his faults, I liked the old devil.'

'I didn't,' I replied bluntly. I bent to unzip the holdall. 'Now . . . that leg of yours. Get back into the sleeping bag, fasten it as high as it will go, but leave the leg out. Hands *inside* the sleeping bag. And a solemn warning, dear Raymond. Anything that even *looks* like trickery, and you'll be able to tell Father how sorry you are . . . personally.'

He did as he was told. Exactly as he was told. I think the leg was giving him hell and that, plus the news of Father had, for the moment knocked all the fight from him. I'd brought what I wanted – what I thought I needed – and the holdall was packed tight with food, drink, plus all I could find for make-do-and-mend surgery. I had no qualms. I'd handled injured animals many times. Mended their wounds and nursed them back to health. Whatever was necessary as far as my half-brother's leg was concerned would be done.

When the coverings had been removed, it was a mess. The bone was set out of alignment; I hoped the two ends had not yet knitted because if they had agony was on the agenda. Where the jaws of the man-trap had smashed into the flesh it looked very nasty indeed. It sported more colours than a rainbow and was swollen to the size of a fist. It also stank. There was pus trapped inside there, and it all had to be released, swabbed out and the flesh made clean. It needed an operating theatre, scalpels and a clinically sterile atmosphere. That's what it needed, but that was something it was not going to *get*.

'There's pain ahead.' I took what I needed from the holdall and placed them on the bench. 'Scream, if you feel like it. It won't stop me. Won't affect me. Scream as loud as you like.'

'That would please you.'

'No.' I removed my outer clothes and rolled up my shirt sleeves. 'Merely that this is going to hurt you a damn sight more than it's going to hurt me.'

'Get on with it. Don't apologise.'

99

I sluiced my hands in Dettol and concentrated on the task. Dettol and iodine. Those were my antiseptics. I cleaned the area with Dettol, dabbed it with iodine then dipped the blade of my knife into Dettol. It was my own knife; razor sharp, but no scalpel, and I knew it would inflict white-hot pain when I used it. He arched his back and his leg muscles trembled, but he made no sound as I opened the putrid flesh a full four inches. The pus, muck and blood came out with a rush. He released his breath with a gasp as the pressure ceased and (I have no doubt) the pain became a 'clean' pain instead of throbbing anguish. I used cotton-wool-tipped cherry sticks to probe and clean the filth from the wound. Like a small mouth, it filled with blood as fast as I cleared it. But I swabbed the filth away, and the flow of blood helped me. I used at least a dozen cherry-sticks – the last two tipped with cotton wool soaked in a mixture of Dettol and iodine – but I was certain the poison had been removed.

I looked up at him for the first time since I'd opened the flesh. He'd passed out. With something of a shock I realised a truth. It is possible to detest a man and still admire him. Not a sound. Not so much as a single moan of pain. My God! I couldn't have done it.

I allowed the blood to flow freely – to cleanse the wound completely – as I threaded the needles. Ordinary sewing needles and ordinary, although strong, nylon thread. I cleaned my hands again, and soaked needles and thread in Dettol before I stitched the lips of the wound together. Eight stitches. Ordinary 'tacking' stitches. I was no surgeon. What I did I did with hope, but in ignorance. I *hoped* I was doing the right thing.

More Dettol. Then Dettol-soaked lint. Then – before the final bandaging – the bone. I straightened it, then packed cotton wool around the whole injury before placing 'splints' of tightly rolled corrugated cardboard into position. It was an improvement on the twigs, especially after I'd fixed things firmly in position with adhesive plaster. Finally, more cotton wool and bandage. I took my time. He could feel nothing. I could fix the foot and leg into an absolutely rigid position. I was quite proud of my handiwork when at last I straightened and examined the end result.

I began to clean up. There was a terrible mess. The sleeping bag and the camp bed were saturated in blood, and that alone took some sluicing off. Blood had soaked into the earth floor of the hut; blood and the poison from the wound. It was obviously alive with bacteria, so I sprinkled Dettol in an attempt to counter the danger. I cleaned my knife and put it away, collected the fouled cherry-sticks and finally rinsed my hands and dried them on cotton-wool. I shrugged on my coat, having rolled down the sleeves of my shirt, and the truth is no heart-transplant surgeon could have felt greater self-satisfaction. The leg was going to heal. I had no doubts. Despite the impossible conditions and the makeshift equipment, I'd done a job of which I was proud.

Murmurings and slight moans were coming from Raymond.

I took a half-bottle of brandy from the holdall, stepped farther into the shelter and eased Raymond into a half-sitting position. I uncorked the brandy and held it to his lips. It brought him round, but for the moment he couldn't speak.

I said, 'The leg inside the sleeping bag. Slowly. Don't undo all the good I've done.'

I unzipped the sleeping bag and helped guide the injured leg into a comfortable position. The damndest thing! At that moment I felt no hatred for him. Only concern. I even trusted him. I was well within reach of his hands – well within attacking distance – yet, instinctively, I knew he would make no attempt. Not merely because he was weak and shock-ridden. It was more than that. For a few moments we shared the same mental wavelength. Don't ask me how or why . . . it just *happened*.

When he was settled, I left him holding the brandy and took food and drink from the holdall and placed it carefully within his reach. Then I sat on the bench and for a few minutes we watched each other in silence.

101

'Father's dead,' he said at last. His voice was weak, but steady. Very sombre. Almost sad. 'All this for nothing. Everything for nothing.'

'I've worked it out.' I matched him, tone for tone. 'His gun, his riding boots. The intention was to kill me, then leave enough evidence to convict *him*.'

'Something like that,' he admitted.

'Involved,' I observed.

'As involved as *this*?'

'I couldn't sit back and let you kill me.'

'No . . . I suppose not.' He moistened his lips with brandy. 'You're quite civilised, aren't you. Odd, but civilised.'

'I like to think so.'

'You could have shot me. Dumped my body here.'

'It never occurred to me.'

'No. That's what I mean.' He shook his head slightly, as if puzzled. 'You could have let this damn leg of mine do it for you.'

'As you say, I'm civilised . . . try to be.'

He screwed the top back onto the bottle and handed it to me.

'Keep it,' I said. 'It gets cool at night.'

'Chilly,' he agreed.

'There's food and hot drinks.' I moved a hand. 'Enough for two days. Maybe three. Inquests, funerals – the usual stuff – I'll be busy for a while.'

He nodded then, softly – almost pleadingly – he said, 'We've gone too far, haven't we? Both of us?'

'Much too far.'

'Two bloody fools,' he sighed sadly.

'Well, one of us is.'

It was a slow walk back to the cottage. A night with little sleep, my experience at the police station, the identification of the body and, finally, the amateur surgery on Raymond's leg had drained me. It was a very slow walk and Sal, who seemed to sense these things, kept at heel obediently and without a whimper of complaint.

The rain was trying to stop. That is the only way to describe it. Trying, but not yet with success; as if the heavens were fighting to stem tears. The cloud cover was complete and the evergreens of the forest still dripped moisture.

On my way home, I hid the gun. It meant a dog-leg from my usual route, but it had to be well hidden. I wrapped it in what was left of the cotton wool and bandages, then secreted it in a hole in the bole of an old oak. The hole couldn't be seen from the ground; to get to it necessitated climbing about ten feet up the trunk – fortunately an easy enough climb – then putting a hand into the hole and lowering the package to elbow-depth. But it was safe. It would never be found.

Guns! Rucker was right, of course. It didn't make him any less obnoxious, but he was right. Too many guns in the world. Too many guns lying around waiting to be picked up by the wrong person. Too many shootings. Too many killings. Too many maimings. Too much violence. Too much madness.

A tired mind in a weary body can find strange paths along which to wander. Dark and haunted paths. Paths leading to frightening places.

I was trembling when I reached the cottage.

I had my second shower of the day, then climbed into bed. A nap . . . or so I thought. I needed rest before tackling the dreary business associated with death and inquests, funerals and empty commiserations.

I must have been tired. Very tired. It was almost two o'clock when the telephone bell awakened me. It was the police. The autopsy had been performed. Death *had* been the result of a massive heart attack. I didn't argue. I'd been drained of all will to argue. The inquest was scheduled for tomorrow at 10.30 a.m. I'd be needed as a witness . . . identification only, of course.

I thanked the caller and hung up.

The calendar on the wall above the telephone. I stared at it for a moment or two. Somehow – somewhere – I seemed to have missed a day. The pressure. The wild activity. The death.

Everything. I checked with *The Radio Times*. A new month had arrived and I'd missed it. It *was* Thursday, November the 2nd. I tore the October page from the calendar and sighed. Bad luck, so the old wives insisted; not to tear the page from a calendar at midnight on the last day of the month was tempting ill-fortune. Like walking under ladders. Like seeing the new moon for the first time through glass.

I'd lived in the country too long. I didn't believe these things. On the other hand, I didn't quite *dis*believe them.

I opened the cottage door to let Sal out, then I returned upstairs to shave and dress. My face was less puffed and the discolouration was fading. The gash on my forehead was knitting. But the pallor was there around what was left of the bruising, and the eyes were sunken and held a wild look. God, I'd been put through the mill . . . and the signs were there.

By three o'clock I was up at the house and, once more, in the midst of it all.

Step-mother was having a whale of a time. Melodrama piled upon melodrama. She was already in black, and gave the impression that she might faint at any moment. Sniffling and crying. Twisting and tearing flimsy handkerchiefs in her restless hands. A caricature from a Bronte novel.

'Such a good man,' she wailed. 'Such a perfect husband. Such a loving father. That he should be . . .'

'The hell he was!' I snapped bluntly.

'Lionel. How can you, of all people . . .'

'How can *you*, of all people,' I countered. 'He led you a dog's life. He led us all a dog's life. He's dead. Damn good riddance to him.'

She ran from the room leaving almost a wake of tears behind her.

'It tends to bring out the worst and the best in us.'

'What?'

I turned to face the stranger. A man of about my own age, but broad and well-built. Dressed in a charcoal-grey suit and sitting quietly in a corner of the room. I didn't know him. I'd

104

noticed him, but thought . . . to be honest, I hadn't thought *anything*. Pre-funeral arrangements meant strangers. Undertakers. Florists. I'd thought . . .

He smiled and said, 'Harvey,' by way of introduction. 'Detective Sergeant Harvey.'

'Oh!'

'Raymond,' he murmured.

'What about Raymond? He's . . .'

I stopped myself in time. Looking back, it sounds crazy. It *was* crazy. I'd been on the point of telling him about the operation on Raymond's leg. That the pus and muck had been removed. That as far as possible . . .

'I'm here instead of Chief Superintendent Rucker,' he cut into my panic-ridden thoughts.

'Quite a . . .' I moistened my lips. Then in a not-very-nice tone, 'Quite a reduction in rank.'

'He's used to giving orders. I'm more used to taking them.'

I returned his smile. He seemed a very pleasant man. Not at all like Rucker. No bombast. No snide. Not at all dangerous . . . not like Rucker had been.

Quietly – almost apologetically – he said, 'It *does* tend to bring out the worst and best. Death. Funerals. That sort of thing.'

'Yes, sergeant, it does,' I agreed.

'I – er – I wasn't meaning to be impertinent.'

'That's quite all right.' Then, because it seemed the right thing to ask, 'Anything new about my half-brother?'

'Nothing you don't know, sir.'

Now, if *Rucker* had made that reply the final 'sir' would not have been included and, at a guess, there might have been some slight emphasis on the second word. As Harvey spoke it, it was a very natural answer to a very obvious question.

Oh yes, I felt quite safe with this Detective Sergeant Harvey.

I had a busy day. I was now, it seemed, surrogate head of the house. Certain decisions had already been provisionally made, subject to my approval. Floral tributes, for example; the mincing clown from the florist's seemed to have been given orders enough to ensure his early retirement.

'A wreath from Step-mother,' I corrected. 'Whatever size or pattern she wants. From the rest of us – from my half-sister, from my half-brother, from myself – just flowers. Bouquets. Nice, but not too fancy. Something we can send to the local hospital after the funeral.'

'And the – er – the other wreaths?'

'What other wreaths?'

'From the estate workers. From the household staff.'

'Cancel them.'

'Lady Cutter was most insistent . . .'

'Lady Cutter,' I said firmly, 'is in no condition to make decisions. I've told you what we want for the immediate family. If the estate workers, or the household staff, wish to contribute wreaths or flowers they'll contact either you or some other florist. But I forbid them to be pressured and, most assuredly, *we* don't foot the bill.'

'He was their employer.' It was a last effort to flog more flowers.

'Did you know my father?' I asked.

'No, sir. I'm afraid . . .'

'In that case, you don't know what the devil you're talking about.'

By which it will be apparent that I felt no loss at the death of my father. The truth is, I felt nothing. Neither sadness nor elation. The unnecessary palaver which seems to accompany all deaths was, if anything, a nuisance. An inconvenience. I wanted it cut down as much as possible . . . and was determined to *have* it cut down. I do not subscribe to the lunatic notion that the act of dying automatically cancels out all previous misdemeanours. In life, Father had been an arrogant, selfish scoundrel. He was no longer alive, but he'd *still* been an arrogant, selfish scoundrel. That was how he would be remembered, and no expensive wall of flowers could block out that memory.

106

Added to which, I hated that house. It held bad memories; memories of tauntings and raging tempers; memories of humiliations and drunken orgies which had disgusted me. Even to walk in that house seemed to stir the echoes of evil. The polished wood of the parquet floors emphasised the clump of my built-up boot. Reminded me that I was as twisted as the house itself. Part of the house. Part of this damned family.

Elizabeth joined me. She wore a navy-blue two-piece and a white blouse. No mock-mourning for her. She was far too honest. Nor did her eyes show signs of weeping. She looked solemn and a little worried.

She said, 'Mother's gone mad.'

'I know,' I grunted. 'I've already crossed swords with the florist.'

'A casket. A hearse and seven cars. Seven!'

'God Almighty!' I took a deep breath. 'Is your car handy?'

'Yes, of course.'

'Drive me to the undertaker's?'

'The – er – "funeral directors".' She shared my disgust.

'Somebody has to slam the brakes on.'

Another man to whom death meant a swelling bank balance. We saw him in his office; an office which would not have shamed a top executive. A rotund man. Fat and oily, with straggling hairs carefully positioned to hide as much of his baldness as possible. A man with a fixed grin of sympathy plastered across his mouth. He waved us to chairs, took up his position behind his desk then clasped his fingers on the desk top in a make-believe posture of half-prayer. His voice was soft, husky . . . as if embarrassed at having to discuss money matters at a time like this. The perfect con man.

I didn't waste time on polite preliminaries.

I said, 'My step-mother instructed you about funeral arrangements for my father.'

'Yes, sir. She said . . .'

'Cancel those instructions.'

He blinked near-disbelief.

'One hearse,' I said. 'Two cars. I doubt if we can fill two cars, but if I'm wrong any hangers-on can drive their own cars.'

'But sir, she was . . .'

'And forget the casket. A coffin. It's going to be burned, so make it reasonable, but not a museum-piece.'

'But sir, he *is* Sir Lioned Cutter.'

'No.' I shook my head. 'He ceased to be Sir Lionel Cutter when he took his last breath. *I'm* Sir Lionel Cutter now.'

'Yes, sir. Of course, sir. But – but the church. The vicar and the arrangements about . . .'

'We'll see the vicar,' I promised him. 'Take these instructions, don't deviate from them without my personal authority. Is that clearly understood?'

'Well – er – yes, sir. But . . .'

'There are no "buts". When the coroner releases the body, box it. Close the lid . . . we want no kissing of corpses. The funeral is – when? – Monday?'

'Monday, at three o'clock, sir.'

'Right. Coffin him, keep him at some Chapel of Rest . . .'

'We have our own, sir.'

'Fine. Keep him there. Arrive at the house in time to reach the crematorium at three. One hearse. Two cars.'

He cleared his throat, then murmured, 'I think your mother will be very upset, sir.'

'Probably,' I snapped. 'But that's *my* worry.'

For some time Elizabeth drove in silence when we left the undertaker's. Her expression was, if not of shock, of surprise. There was, perhaps, a hint of disappointment there, too.

Then quite suddenly and in a soft voice she said, 'You've changed.'

'In what way?' The remark puzzled me.

'You were very assertive. Almost rude.'

'When?' I was still at a loss.

'To the undertaker. He was only doing what he'd been told to do.'

'Oh!'

'You could have been more gentle with him. Less brusque.'

'He's out to make money. They all are.' I found myself defending my attitude, even though I realised she had much truth on her side. 'Widows. Next-of-kin. Normally, they're emotionally incapable of reaching calm decisions. They take advantage.'

'It doesn't follow.'

'Dammit, it's how they grow rich and fat. It's one of the tricks of their trade.'

'Please don't swear.'

'Would *you* like to take over?' It was a stupid question, and the tone of voice was uncalled for.

'No. . .and I'm sorry.' Sorrow and gentleness rode the words.

'Forget it.' It was a muttered, half-apology. A poor thing, but as far as I could bring myself to go. 'I'll see the cleric alone.'

Of course I was wrong and, of course, she was right. The tension and loss of sleep were beginning to tell. A week before – even a day or two before – I wouldn't have handled the undertaker that way. I wouldn't have dared. I'd certainly have been more polite. All my life I'd prided myself on *not* being the lout of the family. Soft, perhaps. Self-conscious. Not given to throwing my weight about.

But now . . .

I saw the parson in the vicarage. In the huge, wall-tiled kitchen of the vicarage, with its massive Aga and huge, deal-topped table. It had been built in an age when incumbents had been expected to 'go forth and multiply'. The whole house a great edifice of multi-roomed, bad-taste Victoriana. This vicar had a wife, but no children. They were as lonely and out of place as two peas rolling around in a barrel.

He apologised for the kitchen.

'It's the one place in this house where you're *sure* to be warm.' He motioned with a hand. 'The Aga, you see. I even write my sermons here in mid-winter.'

'No central heating?' I was taking Elizabeth's advice, and approaching things less bluntly.

109

'I'm not the Archbishop of Canterbury . . . or of York.' He smiled. He had a strangely innocent smile for a middle-aged man. 'Yes, we have central heating. Old fashioned. Solid fuel . . . coke, in fact. So has the church. If *we* use the coke the church is like an ice-box, and the congregation dwindles to nothing. It's rather pointless preaching to empty pews.' He paused, then said, 'You're here because of your father's death, I take it?'

'My step-mother's been in touch with you?'

He nodded.

'What has she arranged?'

'Far too much.' Then hastily, 'She can have it, of course, but I'm glad you came. I – er – I haven't yet arranged for the choir.'

'Don't,' I said gently.

'The bell to be tolled?'

I shook my head.

'Right.' The smile came and went. 'Let's assume Lady Cutter hasn't been in touch with me.'

'Cremation,' I said.

'I'll cancel the grave-diggers.'

'In the family plot,' I said slowly. 'But not for a coffin. For a box – whatever they use – containing the ashes.'

'A short service?'

'Very short. At the crematorium chapel. You, of course.'

'Hymns?'

'I think not. Appropriate music is enough.'

'What do you call appropriate?'

'For him,' I said grimly, 'a ditty called *One-Eyed Riley*. He sang it when drunk . . . you won't know it.'

'Years ago,' he mused, 'I used to play rugby. Yes, I know the song. Even the dirty version.'

'The dirty version is *very* appropriate.'

'But not available, I'm afraid.'

'Pity.'

He eyed me wisely – perhaps sadly – for a moment, then said, 'It isn't often one meets a man who hates his father as

110

much as you do.'

'You didn't know him.'

'No.'

'And,' I said, 'a father-hating son is against all you stand for.'

'Is it?' He raised a quizzical eyebrow.

'Mere earthly sins . . . all that stuff.'

'I don't preach that. Don't believe it. That particular worn-out theological doctrine puts me on a par with Hitler. With Stalin. With *real* sinners. I may not be Persil-white, but I have my good points . . . and I'll argue that with The Almighty Himself.'

I grinned. The first real feeling of cheerfulness for a long time. This cleric was a man I could grow to like.

He said, '*Solemn Melody*. The Watford Davies piece.'

'If you think so,' I agreed.

'Very dirge-like. Well known, but not hackneyed. They have a record of it at the crematorium chapel. They usually bung it on for atheists and agnostics.'

'Fine.' I stood up and held out my hand. 'Three o'clock, Monday.'

'I'll be there . . . looking suitably solemn.'

We shook hands and I left the vicarage and joined Elizabeth in the car. As I climbed in beside her, my expression must have reflected my change of mood.

'*Not* a confrontation this time,' she murmured.

'With men like that around, there's hope for religion yet.'

All that day, all the following day (Friday) it seemed I hadn't time to pause long enough to eat a proper meal. Up at the house; the place I hated most in the world. Coping with a crazy step-mother who seemed determined to make the funeral the event of the year; arguing with her; demanding that she see Father for what he'd been, and not for what she *wished* he'd been. Answering a thousand stupid questions from various members of the household staff. Checking with the estate manager at the estate office. Telephoning the solicitor.

111

Telephoning the accountant. The truth is, I hadn't realised that having wealth necessitated so much decision making.

With Step-mother in such a state and Father dead the household staff were disorganised. It had never been one of those Upstairs–Downstairs, smooth-running set-ups; the 'turnover in servants had played havoc with any hope of 'old retainer' continuity. Now it was minor chaos.

I took Elizabeth to one side.

'You're the boss,' I said bluntly.

'I – I can't. I haven't . . .'

'You can and you have. Look, forget sentimentality. *I* am now Sir Lionel Cutter, like it or lump it. I'm putting you in charge of the house. Don't tell them . . . *order* them. It's what they're used to.' Then in a burst of irritation, 'Good God, he's causing more trouble dead than he did alive.'

Then I returned to the cottage, assured Sal she hadn't been forgotten and took her for a short stroll through the trees.

I slept fitfully. Badly. Twice during that Thursday night I climbed from my bed to stand at the window and stare at my beloved forest. The moon was a mere three days old, but it was there above the trees, a silver scimitar making its monthly appearance. Slim, sharp-edged gainst a blue-black background. I'd seen it so many times. The representation of never-changing eternity. Aloof, cold and very beautiful. I had no yen to walk its surface. No desire to probe its mystery. All I wanted – all I'd ever wanted – was it to be *there* and visible from my cottage window.

But now . . .

I wept quietly. Silently. I wept for my moon and for my forest. For my sky and for my trees. For the things I loved and the squalid circumstances which were combining to tear them from my grasp. Peace! In God's name why was I being denied mere peace? Peace of mind. Was solitude and the right to be left alone so great a thing to ask? A book to read, music to listen to, an occasional visit from Elizabeth. That's all I wanted. Not 'Sir' before my name. Not to have to argue with money-

112

grabbing florists and undertakers. He was dead. Bury him, burn him . . . anything. But, above all, forget him. Equally, forget *me*. Leave me alone. Allow me to enjoy my simple pleasures without the fear of death – or, if not death, prison – hanging over me. I was no criminal. In all my life, I had never done a deliberate wrong. Nobody could point the finger of vengeance at me. Self-preservation, perhaps. A determination, of a sort, to remain alive.

Mixed thoughts, all of them bad. A dozen impossible questions, none of which had a sane answer. They denied me quiet sleep and made me miserable.

Friday, of course, saw the inquest. It was a new experience for me, and one I could have done without. The coroner was a loathsome man. Not deliberately, I think, but because it was 'his' court and he obviously counted it as part of his duty to be forever reminding those present of that fact. 'Unless you are giving evidence you will remain seated, unless I say otherwise' . . . this to an obviously terrified young police constable who'd left his seat to close a window. Then almost immediately afterwards, 'I find this room uncomfortably chilly. Somebody close that window.'

The whole inquest was punctuated by such ridiculous utterances. He was king of this particular castle and found perverse pleasure in emphasising that fact.

The pathologist – a woman, I was surprised to discover – gave her evidence. She used medical jargon, but what she meant was that Father had suffered a massive heart attack.

'Due to what?' asked the coroner.

'I'm not able to say. Merely that that was the cause of his death.'

'I'm told he had an ungovernable temper.'

'I didn't know him, sir.'

'Could *that* have brought on a heart attack?'

'It's possible.'

'Be more specific.'

'I performed an autopsy.' She, too, was showing impatience. 'I have given evidence of my findings. What caused his death. What led up to that cause would be pure speculation.'

The coroner scowled annoyance, but left it at that.

The poor constable who'd been on cell duty took what the coroner had been unable to throw at the pathologist.

'You say he was shouting?'

'Yes, sir.'

'Why was he shouting?'

'He was locked in a cell, sir. It made him angry.'

'He'd been arrested, hadn't he?'

'Yes, sir.'

'Justifiably?'

'Yes, sir.'

'Then, why was he angry?'

'I – I don't know, sir. Because he'd been locked up.'

'Didn't you explain things to him?'

'Sir?'

'Tell him *why* he was locked in a cell?'

'He was told why he'd been arrested, sir.'

'By you?'

'By Chief Superintendent Rucker, sir. I was there when he was told.'

'Did he understand?'

'Yes, sir. I'm sure he did.'

'Then, why was he angry?'

'I don't know, sir.'

'Why was he shouting?'

'I don't know, sir.'

'The man must have been mad.'

'Yes, sir.'

'You mean he *was* mad?'

'He was – he was very angry, sir. Very outraged. He refused to be quietened.'

'Quite mad.'

That infernal word. The constable's cross-examination by this popinjay coroner continued, and the unfortunate officer was badgered mercilessly, but a humming then a roaring dynamo seemed to fill my head with noise, and I was unable to concentrate. It seemed that five – probably ten – minutes were removed from my life. I saw nothing, heard nothing, was conscious of nothing. A gap. Something the science fiction writers might call a 'time slip'. It wasn't that I was unconscious or even dead. It went farther than that. For that short space of time it was as if I'd never been born.

I 'came back' (the only way I can express it) as the constable left the witness box and I heard my own name called.

I walked to the witness box a little unsteadily. A kindly sergeant touched my elbow, but I shook him off. Then I took the oath and gave evidence that I had identified the corpse as that of my father.

'What sort of a man was he?' asked the coroner.

'I didn't know him too well.'

'He was your father, wasn't he?'

'We didn't live in the same house.'

'Why was that?'

'We had different opinions . . . about everything.'

'You had disagreements?'

'Not often.'

'You've just said . . .'

'We didn't see each other often enough to have many disagreements.' I paused, then added, 'We didn't like each other.'

'Really? Why was that?'

This self-important little man needed chopping down to size and, in my present mood, I was going to enjoy doing it.

I said, 'You have used the word "mad". You forced that constable to suggest that my father was "mad". I don't know. *You* don't know. Certainly the constable doesn't know . . .'

'Are you suggesting . . .'

'... But one thing I do know. Had my father undergone psychological or psychiatric treatment – had he been examined by experts – I doubt if he would have been pronounced completely sane. I don't know what the definition of true madness is. To that extent I will not be brow-beaten into expressing a firm and unqualified opinion. Merely that he wasn't normal – wasn't stable – *but few of us are, are we?*'

I glanced to my left. The half-dozen or so reporters had their heads bent and were scrawling furiously in their notebooks. They now had something to write about.

Without being told, without waiting for permission, I left the witness box, left the room and flopped onto a bench on the passage. What happened inside the court-room I don't know. Nor do I care.

I sat there for about five minutes, then the door opened and the chief constable joined me. I hadn't even noticed him among the other uniformed figures. He sat down alongside me, opened a packet of cigarettes and held it towards. I took one. I hadn't smoked for five years. I'd fought and kicked the habit but, at that moment, that cigarette seemed to be a life-saver. He flicked a lighter into flame and, when the cigarettes were lighted, blew a stream of smoke towards the ceiling.

'Neat,' he murmured.

'I'm sorry?'

'Telling the old bugger he was crazy, without using those exact words.'

The unaccustomed cigarette smoke caught at my throat, stung a little but didn't make me cough.

The chief constable said, 'Cause of death. Satisfied?'

'Why not?'

'I've made enquiries. Nobody was with him. Nobody put a foot wrong.'

'I believe you.' I believed him, but I didn't care.

'Sergeant Harvey?' He drew on his cigarette. 'We still have the kidnapping.'

'Harvey's fine.'

116

'This alters things slightly,' he said, slowly.

'What?'

'*You're* Sir Lionel Cutter now.'

'Oh!'

'The ransom . . . that side of things.'

'Let things stand till this lot's over,' I sighed.

He nodded, and we smoked in silence.

Back at the house the atmosphere was as miserable and as cold as the mortuary in which lay Father's body. Dark, echoing and lifeless, and no place for me in my present mood.

'Are you going back to the cottage?' Elizabeth seemed to read my mind.

I nodded.

'May I come with you?'

'Why not? You look as if some fresh air might do you good.'

We walked slowly for a while, then she murmured, 'I wonder if Raymond knows?'

'What?'

'About Father's death.'

'I think so.' It was like treading, barefoot, through nettles. 'If he doesn't now, he soon will. Enough reporters were at the inquest.'

'If they let him see a newspaper.'

'Why shouldn't they?'

'I know so little about these things.'

'They asked me if I thought Father was mad.' I changed the subject.

'Who?'

'At the inquest.'

'Oh!' She looked startled. 'What did you say?'

'That he might have been.'

'Lionel!'

'It's true, isn't it? The way he behaved, sometimes.'

'Eccentric,' she murmured gently. 'I'd have said eccentric.'

'Because he's dead,' I said flatly. 'I've seen him hurt people, for the sake of hurting them. I've seen you in tears, for no reason at all. That's not eccentricity.'

The talk continued as we strolled. It added up to very little. There was a corpse between us; alive he'd been intolerable, dead he was an embarrassment. There was also a captive between us, but she didn't know that.

We reached the cottage, and I let Sal out for a run. Meanwhile, we made a snack, then relaxed and listened to music. Sal returned and I fed and watered her, and she was happy again. A scene of domesticity, but only mock-domesticity. The fantasy warmth of a lighthouse surrounded by storm-wracked seas. We made-believe. It was the only thing we had left.

I slept well that night. If my conscience should have troubled me, it certainly did not. Perhaps I had no conscience. No sense of guilt. Since I began the recording of those events of 1978 I've often wondered. Try as I might I cannot *remember* any feeling of guilt. Disgust, yes. An occasional flash of anger. But in the main, sorrow. I was a creature of circumstances, and I had no control over those circumstances. They hammered me this way and that, and forced me to do things of which I am now ashamed. But, I repeat, they *forced* me. I was given no option. I handled the truth as well as I was able, but I was damned if I was going to die for the sake of a petty and undeserved title. I wasn't going to die, and I wasn't going to starve. Surely, a reasonable enough attitude to take? Perhaps that's why I slept deeply and without dreams.

I awakened at dawn. That was the Saturday, November the 4th; a cold but bright morning, and ideal for a brisk walk through the trees. I breakfasted, packed the holdall and set out, with Sal as my companion.

We dog-legged to pick up the revolver. It seemed a necessary precaution. He'd had two full days in which to think up some scheme to either free himself or cause some sudden harm to me. He wouldn't have wasted that time. I made no self-pretence. I daren't. He was quietened, perhaps, but he wasn't tamed.

I called to him from behind the screen of undergrowth.

He answered and, before I could tell him, he was struggling from his bed and to a sitting position on the bench. He even opened the conversation.

'It's been a long time.'

'Necessary.' I showed myself and took up my position by the birch, with Sal on top of the bank, watching. 'The inquest and all the arrangements for the cremation.'

'You're burning him?'

'It seems an appropriate end.'

'Probably so.'

Odd. His voice was calm. The tone held no hatred. Not even dislike. I mistrusted that tone. It was too philosophical for my peace of mind.

'The inquest?' he asked.

'He died from a heart attack.' I hesitated, then added, 'They asked if I thought he was mad.'

'And?'

'I said he might have been.'

'He was. Mad as a hatter.'

'You knew him better than I did.'

'He was mad.' He sighed, then moved his mouth into a crooked smile. '*He* was mad. *I'm* mad. *You're* mad. Elizabeth. We're a mad family . . . haven't you realised that, yet?'

'How's the leg?' I asked.

'Much better. You missed your vocation. You should have been a surgeon.'

'A terrifying thought,' I taunted gently. 'A mad doctor.'

'Why not? Most of them are.'

With something of a shock I realised that I was accepting the proposition that I was mad – that the whole family was off its collective rocker – with easy equanimity.

Somewhere (I forget where) I'd read that the proverbial

119

'normal man' doesn't exist. That he is a creation of the shrink fraternity; a fictitious base-line from which to determine sub-normality and abnormality. Nor (if I remember correctly) was the theory voiced by some crank. The author of the article was a highly-respected mind expert and the article was published in a well-thought-of publication. The 'ordinary' then, is not there. We are all more than 'ordinary' or less than 'ordinary' Which, I suppose, means we all have traits which, in turn, makes us all individuals.

'Does it scare you?' asked Raymond gently.

'What?'

'That the Cutters are all off their head? That the blood's rotten?'

'No,' I said slowly, 'it doesn't scare me. I'm sorry I'm part of it – if I *am* part of it – but it doesn't scare me.'

'You're part of it, boy,' he insisted. 'This present situation.' He moved his hands. 'Is *this* sane? Is what led up to it sane?'

'You were out to kill me,' I reminded him.

'Sure. Two tries. Two misses. Is *that* sane?'

'Catch.' I tossed the still-zipped holdall towards him and he caught it without difficulty. 'Food, fruit, water, soup and tea. I'll be back tomorrow with more.'

'Don't go.' He unzipped the holdall and placed the contents carefully on the bench alongside him. 'Talk a little.'

'What about?'

'Anything. It gets lonely out here.'

'I'm never lonely.'

'Just for a while,' he pleaded.

I squatted down with my back against the birch. Why not? This was my environment. I was content enough to be here, and away from the house.

'Have they missed me?' he asked.

'Of course.'

'What conclusions have they come to?'

'You've been kidnapped.'

He was raising an apple to his mouth, and he stopped half-way there and stared.

'Kidnapped for a ransom,' I expounded. 'They got the usual letter.'

'*You* sent it?'

'Who else?'

He bit into the apple and munched for a moment.

'What am I worth? he asked.

'Half a million.'

'Cheap at the price.' He chuckled softly. 'Will they pay?'

'Father might not have.'

'Ah, but now *you're* the king of the castle.'

'I'll pay,' I said gently.

'Pay yourself?'

'I'll see it gets paid.' There was a subtle difference. 'Then you'll be free.'

He took a second bite of the apple, chewed then swallowed before he spoke again.

'Okay, you've paid yourself half a million. I'm free. What happens then?'

I moved my shoulders and waited.

He placed the half-eaten apple alongside him on the bench, lifted a Thermos from the holdall and unscrewed the top. He spoke as he poured tea. It might have been a quiet conversation in a gentleman's club. Polite. Without rancour. Without a hint of emotion.

'We'll be back to square one. A little more care this time. A little more cunning. You'll be watching your back for the rest of your life . . . and, one day, you *won't* be watching.'

'To say nothing of the police,' I smiled.

'No police.' He sipped tea, then shook his head. 'I don't want you in prison, boy. I want you dead.'

'From where you're sitting,' I smiled, 'that is a particularly foolish remark to make.'

'You won't kill me.' He sounded so sure . . . and he was so right.

I allowed him to eat and drink in silence for some time. For the life of me (*literally* for the life of me!) I couldn't hate him. I tried – tried to see him as my would-be murderer – but it was no good. I hadn't it in me. He was there, unshaven, dirty, injured, chained . . . yet there was a rapport between us which had never been present before. I couldn't follow his reasoning. To use his own expression it was 'mad' reasoning. Yet he believed it and spoke what he thought was the truth . . . and that of itself took courage.

I said, 'The police are already investigating the kidnapping. Father called them in from the start.'

'That must be interesting for you.'

'For a time it was uncomfortable,' I admitted.

He laughed aloud.

'You find it so funny?' I asked.

'Just that they won't learn the truth from me. Okay, I've been kidnapped, but I don't know who kidnapped me.'

'There's a man called Rucker,' I murmured.

'Who?'

'Detective Chief Superintendent Rucker. *He'll* screw the truth out of you.'

'I want you alive, old son. I don't want you tucked away in some jail.'

'Alive?'

'For my own amusement.'

'Will it be so amusing?' I asked a little bitterly. 'Will it be worth the risk?'

I waited. He didn't answer for some time. He chewed, swallowed and sipped, and I began to think he wasn't going to answer. That there was no answer, or at least no adequate answer he could come up with.

Then he wiped the back of a hand across his mouth and spoke quietly, but very sincerely.

'This little lot.' He waved his hand. His tone was amiable enough, but I knew he meant every word. 'You trapped me like a rabbit in a gin. Smashed my leg. Brought me here and chained me like an animal. I live and sleep in my own filth.

122

Defecate in a hole in the ground. I'm fed and watered at your pleasure. You think that makes for brotherly love, boy? You thing I'm not going to even the balance? All this is doing is making damn *sure*. I'm going to get amusement. I'm going to get *pleasure*.'

'I could have killed you,' I reminded him.

'Oh, no.' He shook his head and smiled. 'You *could* have, but you didn't. You're not the killing kind, boy. You think *this* is better than killing. More humane. A trapped animal – an injured animal – you'll put it through hell to make it whole again. It would prefer death. A quick death. But that's something you don't understand. You'll end up telling them where I am, and I'll end up telling them nothing. After that, you'll be the hunted and I'll be the hunter. But that game leg of yours, that bent back of yours, won't fool me for a third time. You're whole. You're complete, boy. You've taught me that. But I've hunted stag . . . and killed them. You too, *Sir* Lionel Cutter. I'll do the same to you.'

He emptied the holdall, re-zipped it and tossed it back to me.

I began making these notes – telling this story – in fine form. But as the memories flood back it becomes more dificult. The *real* memories. The *true* emotions. They are real, but sound unreal. When I began, I thought they were stereotyped, but they're not. They're not what they should be.

A man you once loathed, you now admire. A man who calmly promises to murder you. You should hate him. At the very least have some fear of him. But, no! No hatred. No fear. No brotherly love . . . a million miles from that. But something new. Something troublesome.

A form of respect, perhaps. An acknowledgement of courage. In a strange way, he'd *proved* himself. He still wasn't the sort of man I'd ever befriend or even like. But he was a *man*. To that extent there was merit in him. Therefore a form of nobility I could not deny. The nobility of the hard-as-nails street fighter; giving no quarter, asking no quarter; refusing to accept the bare possibility of defeat.

Previously – before I'd captured and chained him – I'd thought him nasty and weak. How wrong. How monumentally wrong! He had a personal pride which astounded me. Courage and a strength of character I'd never dreamed of.

As I walked home that day I was forced to re-appraise my previous opinion of this half-brother of mine. It wasn't easy; to give grudging credit is never easy. But credit was there and I gave him full measure.

I left Sal and the holdall at the cottage, changed into shoes and continued up to the house. Detective Sergeant Harvey was still there.

'Don't you *ever* go off duty?' I asked.

'Orders.' He smiled. 'I'm a single man. Nobody is waiting for me.'

I thought it wise to continue the kidnapping charade.

'You think they'll still contact us?' I asked.

'They'll know your father's dead. The newspapers carried the inquest findings.'

'That's what I mean.'

'If they contact anybody it will be you.'

'That will be a waste of time,' I said bluntly.

He raised questioning eyebrows.

'Where do *I* find half a million pounds?' I amplified.

'They'll probably wait until after the will's been read.'

I grunted, left him and clumped farther into the house. My God, that house! That was something I *did* hate and always will. The rooms; too many of them; each too large to be cosy, but too small to command admiration; the proportions were all wrong and whoever designed it was a fool. And passages; passages for the sake of passages; passages left, as if to fill the space between the outer walls. A would-be country mansion carved up into ill-sized boxes with spaces between.

I rounded a corner and almost collided with Elizabeth.

'Oh!'

'I'm sorry,' I apologised.

'No . . . that's all right.' She waved her hands a little, in near-despair. She looked pale and harassed. 'I – er – I have to tell you. They've telephoned. The solicitors . . . they telephoned. We haven't to touch anything until after the will.'

'What?'

'Y'know . . . until they've read the will.'

'Great heavens,' I exploded, 'do they think we're going to pawn the family silver?'

'It's – it's the way it's done.' She pushed a lock of straying hair back into position. 'They were polite enough. Just that . . .'

'Forget it.' I looked at her closely. Then in a quiet, but determined tone, I said, 'Forget everything. We're going out.'

'Lionel, we can't. There's . . .'

'There's nothing,' I insisted. 'You look shattered. It's all been done. We need a break. *You* need a break.'

'Mother's being very difficult,' she muttered miserably.

'Fine. She can be difficult in her own time for a few hours.'

'Lionel . . . we *can't.*'

'The pictures.' I wasn't going to take a negative answer. 'A good film, then a nice meal. If they want us – *anybody* – they can jump up and down till we get back.'

'D-dare we?' she breathed.

'We're *going* to.'

The film? I forget the film . . . I think it was a re-run of *Where Eagles Dare*. I know Elizabeth had seen it before, and I wasn't too interested, but the choice was that or soft porn served up in varying guises. It was at Bordfield and we sat in the half-empty auditorium, and our fingers linked almost automatically, and I felt her presence as never before, and I relaxed and was almost happy.

Almost! That 'almost' represented the blood-tie. A few months previously, had anybody asked me, I would have said (*and* meant) that women were not for me. No woman. I'd die an unmarried man. Bachelorhood was as much a part of my life as eating or sleeping and I'd never change.

I'd have sworn to that. It was what I'd wanted. The only thing I'd wanted.

But now . . .

Getting to know Elizabeth had changed things. Reversed things . . . except they *couldn't* be reversed. Happily, I would have given ten years of my life for us not to have been half-brother and half-sister. Damn that step-mother of mine. Why had she to marry *my* father? Why not some stranger, then . . .

Then, I might not have met Elizabeth, and what happiness I had might have been denied me.

Like a child's kaleidoscope, the patterns and colours changed as I turned the thoughts which filled my mind. But always a tiny part of the pattern was missing. The colour was never complete.

We had supper at a quiet little restaurant. The table was private and nobody could see or hear us, and things had to be said. I reached a hand across the table and closed my fingers over hers as I spoke.

'Elizabeth . . .' I began, then choked for a moment. Then, 'If I could, I'd ask you to marry me.'

She lowered her head a little.

'You should know that.' I grew a little bolder. 'In fairness, you should know. No other woman . . . ever. Only you.'

'I'm . . . proud,' she whispered.

'You've known, surely? You've known for a long time.'

She nodded, without raising her head.

'If . . .' Then I stopped. Having said what I wanted to say, I didn't know how to go on. I squeezed her hand gently.

'Stupid mores.' Her voice was as hoarse and as sad as mine. 'Stupid people. There was a time in history . . .'

'Not *our* time, darling.'

'A more civilised time. A more understanding time.'

'Perhaps.'

For all of fifteen seconds she stared at the table-cloth. She wanted to say something, but couldn't. Didn't know how. Couldn't find the words. Then when, at last, she spoke the words came out on a trembling breath.

'If – if you want me to.'

'What?' I stared.

'Later . . . when you go home. I'll – I'll stay.'

'Darling, I'm not . . .'

'Please, Lionel!' The words were so low – so whispered – her lips hardly moved. 'It's – it's not meant to be a sacrifice. A gesture. I – I *want* to sleep with you . . . if that's what *you* want.'

'No!' The word was out – said, and in a flat, hard voice – before I could hold it back. I squeezed her hand tightly. Communicating with her. Forcing her to understand. I wanted to say 'Yes' . . . God, how I wanted to say 'Yes'. Instead, I said, 'The whole or nothing, my pet. What we have – what we already have – is more than most couples can ever claim. We'd debase it. We'd spoil it.' I took a deep breath, and let it out in a long, sad sigh. 'To be your husband . . . *anything* to be your husband. But the other thing. We'd regret it.'

'I – I don't think . . .'

'We *might* regret it,' I insisted. 'We'd both know we'd done something wrong. Broken the law, even. I won't risk it. I won't risk what I already have.' I moistened my lips, then added, 'Of course I'd like to go to bed with you. To make love to you. Of *course*. Do I have to tell you? But after that, what? Guilt, perhaps? A feeling of shame? I won't risk it, darling. I *daren't* risk it. I might lose what I already have . . . a thing far too precious to lose.'

She raised her head, looked at me and smiled. Such a sad smile. A single tear spilled from one eye and crept down her cheek.

Such nobility. Such *bloody* nobility!

All that night, all next day (Sunday) I tortured myself. I didn't know women. Even Elizabeth. I didn't even *pretend* to know her. She'd been silent and a little withdrawn on the way home, and the parting had been the usual touch of lips on the forehead.

127

So, had my ham-handed declining of her offer been an insult? Had I offended her? My reasons were both honest and honourable, but she was no whore. She'd offered the most precious thing she had, and I'd turned it down.

What was I, then? A gentleman or a lout? I was a man in love. Crazy in love. But in love with a woman who could never be my wife. Never! So, why not settle for the other thing? It wasn't a matter of waiting. A matter of divorce or even death. God, I'd have waited forever . . . but it wasn't a matter of waiting. She'd *always* be my half-sister. The same blood. The same parent. The same father.

On the Sunday I drove out and bought cigarettes. The first time for years. I'd kicked the habit. Heart attacks, lung cancer. I'd been convinced . . . but it didn't matter any more. Nicotine was a drug, and I wanted *something*. I also bought Scotch. A hundred cigarettes and two bottles of whisky.

I packed the holdall tight with food and drink. It had to last two days . . . and Raymond was becoming a damn nuisance. Every day – at best every alternate day – he had to be fed and watered. Something I hadn't thought of. Hadn't bargained for.

I shoved the Smith and Wesson in my mac pocket. Why? Well maybe on that day, of all days, I'd blow his stupid head off if he tried to smart-talk me too much. *That* day. The only day I ever seriously contemplated the possibility of murder.

He didn't. He was strangely quiet.

As he emptied the holdall, he said, 'Tomorrow.'

'What?'

'The funeral. The cremation.'

I grunted an affirmative reply.

'I'd like to have been there,' he sighed.

'Crap.'

'It's getting at you.' He stared at my glowering face and frowned. 'Even you. It's getting at . . .'

'What the hell are you talking about?' I snarled.

'The old man's sudden death.'

I almost laughed aloud. So wrong. So utterly wrong.

128

'Don't tell me it didn't affect you.' He was quite meticulous in the way he arranged the parcels, packages, bottles and vacuums on the bench. 'Don't tell me you felt *nothing*.'

'I was sorry,' I grunted.

He nodded, knowingly.

'That he died so quickly,' I added. 'The old devil should have suffered a few days of agony. It's what he deserved.'

'You really *hated* him.' For some reason he sounded surprised.

'And you. Both of you,' I agreed.

'Me, I can understand. But . . .'

'Little brother, you are nothing.' The contempt and bitterness coloured my words, but it was a bitterness the cause of which he was unaware. 'You tell me to watch my back. For the rest of my life. I walk away from here, forget you . . . and I *can* forget you. You've been kidnapped. If you're never seen again, who'll be surprised? It wouldn't be unique. It happens to many kidnap victims.'

'We were talking about Father,' he reminded me gently.

'Reasons,' I said harshly. 'Many reasons. Recently an extra reason. A very important reason.'

'What?'

'You wouldn't understand. I'm not going to tell you.'

'Just leave me here to die?'

'Maybe.'

'You won't do that.' He shook his head as he spoke.

'Don't bet the Cutter fortune on it.'

He chuckled and said, 'Two days' supply of food and drink?'

'So?'

'You're keeping me alive, boy. You don't keep somebody alive if you intend killing them.'

'It's a thought,' I said wearily. 'Hang onto it.'

3 p.m., Monday November 6th, 1978. A time and a day to remember. The chapel was almost empty; the family, the solicitor and a couple of the house servants. A true measure of

129

the man's popularity and, as the coffin slid between the curtains, I felt nothing. He'd gone. A whisp of smoke and a handful of grey ash . . . the late Sir Lionel Cutter.

The cleric had chosen his words well. 'He will be missed by all who knew him.' 'He died suddenly, in the prime of life, but we must give thanks that he was spared a lingering and painful death.' I found myself wondering how long it had taken him to compose even a short sermon which told the truth without actually saying 'good riddance'.

Then we trooped from the chapel, climbed into the cars and made our way home.

We shared the same car. Elizabeth, Step-mother and I. On the way to the service we hadn't spoken. The tension was there. Perhaps the tension which accompanies all funerals. Step-mother had sniffled conscientiously. Elizabeth had stared from the car window. I had closed my eyes; I'd had little sleep the previous night, I'd tippled a mite too much whisky and I was content to remind myself that, within the next hour or so, the facade would be over. On the way back, the tension had eased and I lighted a cigarette.

Elizabeth glanced at me and looked surprised.

'I thought you didn't . . .'

'I've started again. I need it. I also need a stiff drink . . . but that must wait.'

'Oh!'

'Foolish things. Stupid things.' For some God-only-knows reason I wanted to hurt her. 'Opportunities lost. Offers rejected, when they should have been accepted.'

'What are you two talking about?' asked Step-mother.

'Something you know nothing at all about.'

Very gently, Elizabeth said, 'You usually make wise decisions.'

'Do I?' My tone was without emotion.

'What *are* you talking about?'

'Fairy tales.' My voice was less harsh. 'But not the Hans Andersen style. More like the Brothers Grimm.'

130

'I still don't know what . . .'

'Mother, it doesn't matter.' Elizabeth glanced at me and a quick smile touched her lips, and I knew my world *hadn't* ended after all. 'It's something Lionel and I witnessed on Saturday evening. In a restaurant. Two people, very much in love. One lost her head. The other *kept* his. He was quite a wonderful man.'

'Oh!'

'He'll live to regret it,' I said simply.

'I doubt it.' The quick smile came and went. 'But *she* might have.'

'I never stare at people in restaurants. It's bad manners.'

'Quite, Mother.' She patted Step-mother's arm comfortingly. 'But sometimes you can't help it. You're too close.'

It reminded me of a small-time conjuring act. The occasional table placed strategically in the library, with the solicitor seated behind it; the 'conjurer' about to perform his little tricks of manipulation. The audience – Step-mother, Elizabeth, myself and a handful of estate and house servants – seated in a half-circle of chairs all waiting to be baffled by some tin-pot jiggery-pokery. It was, of course, the Reading of the Will. A most anticipatory moment . . . except for myself who, thanks to Eric's drunken talk, knew that the person about to collect the jackpot wasn't present.

Eric was there. He sat alongside the senior partner of the firm, ready to fetch and carry as he was instructed. The senior partner was a large man; florid-faced with a bulbous nose road-mapped with tiny blue veins. He had a voice to suit his body. A rich, fruity voice. A ham-actor's voice. He declaimed rather than spoke; wrapping every word in juicy confection before he allowed it past his lips.

As he placed thick, horn-rimmed spectacles into place across his face, Eric hoisted the leather satchel from alongside his chair and placed it on the table.

'Ladies and gentleman, may I have your attention, please.'

131

He rolled the words out as he unbuckled the straps holding the flap of the satchel. 'It is now my duty to read the will of the late Sir Lionel Cutter. It is not a very lengthy document. Nor is it too involved.' He drew a folded parchment from the satchel, and Eric removed the satchel from the table. 'Nevertheless usage – indeed, the law – requires me to read it aloud in its entirety. After I have read the will – and only then – I will, as far as possible, clarify any points which might be raised.'

He settled the spectacles more firmly into position and cleared his throat. I relaxed in my chair and pretended to listen. Pretended, because my thoughts were elsewhere. Remembering a restaurant and a table where a gauche, deformed man was tempted and was, perhaps, a coward. Remembering a man, once hated but now commanding reluctant admiration, whose greed for a baronetcy had resulted in him being chained like an animal and removed from civilised society. Remembering what that same man had said about madness. About the inherent madness of the whole Cutter family. And wondering. Pondering upon the possible truth of that observation.

'This is the last will and testament of me Sir Lionel Cutter, baronet . . . hereby revoke all former wills and other testamentory dispositions at any time heretofore made by me . . . to my wife, Lady Grace Cutter, and that the said monies be invested by my trustee in such a manner as to ensure that the said Lady Grace Cutter remains free from debt and lives in a manner to which she is accustomed . . . to my daughter, Elizabeth Cutter, and that the said monies be invested by my trustee in such a manner as to ensure . . . that the said Lady Grace Cutter and my daughter Elizabeth Cutter be allowed to live at the above mentioned address free and without restraint of any kind so long as either so wish . . . to my estate manager . . . to my housekeeper . . . to my elder son, Lionel Cutter, I give devise and bequeath all other monies, all bonds and shares, the whole of my real and personal estate whatsoever and wheresoever situate and of whatsoever nature and

132

kindsoever . . . To my younger son, Raymond Cutter, I devise and bequeath nothing . . . that, in so doing, he may be encouraged to handle shotguns with more care and less criminal negligence . . . in witness thereof I have set my hand this tenth day of August, nineteen hundred and seventy eight.' He raised his hand, eased the spectacles lower on his nose in order to peer at me above the frames, then smiled and rumbled, 'Congratulations, Sir Lionel. You are a very rich man.'

Rich! Dear God, even after the tax man had had his bite, I had far more money than I could spend in a lifetime. I owned land by the square mile. Farms. Whole villages. I had controlling shares in more than half-a-dozen companies, and lesser shares in a score more.

And the secret?

The date of the will. A few days after I'd stormed into the house asking for Jem to be given his job back, and that was the day I'd left Father in no doubt about Raymond's first attempt to murder me. Once more he'd changed his will . . . and this time for the last time.

I stayed around for the usual ritual of sherry and snacks, but as soon as possible I excused myself and walked slowly back to the cottage. Elizabeth caught up with me when I was about half way home and fell into step alongside me. I smiled a welcome, but we walked in silence for a few minutes.

Then in a low voice she said, 'So it *was* true, after all?'

'What?'

'Raymond *did* try to kill you?'

'Yes.' I kicked at a short length of twig on the path, but because of my built-up shoe missed completely.

'Why?' she asked.

'He wanted the title. To be *Sir* Raymond Cutter.' I pushed my hands deep into the pockets of my trousers. 'He was greedy. Prior to this last will he'd been left everything. It wasn't enough.'

'How do you . . .'

133

'Eric told me.' I forestalled her question. 'Eric, the young chap with the solicitor. He has a big mouth, and he was a little drunk.' We walked a few steps in silence. 'I didn't mind. Had I been able to give it to him, he could have had the damn title. And the money. I'd have worked something out.'

It was a lie, of course. I'd decided to 'remove' Raymond within minutes of Eric telling me of the will-change . . . and from that decision everything else had flowed. But that did not matter. I was wealthy. I had power. And when the powerful speak, they speak the truth, even when they lie in their teeth.

As I opened the cottage door and stood aside to allow her to pass, she said, 'Why should he do that?'

'Who?'

'Father. Why should he leave everything to Raymond and nothing to you?'

'Look at me,' I suggested. I closed the door, followed her into the cottage, bent to scratch Sal's ears, then we both flopped into our respective chairs. 'I, as eldest son, was expected to continue the Cutter line. Me! A deformed recluse. A man with no interest whatever in hunting, shooting or fishing. Assuming some woman knew me well enough to marry me . . .'

'*Loved* you well enough to marry you.'

'That would be asking too much.'

'Lionel, that's not a nice thing to say.'

'Ah, but *we* don't count.' I smiled at her. 'We're two of the "different" people. We love each other *despite* . . . not *because*.'

'You're a better man than Father ever was.'

'Probably . . . but that isn't saying much. Nor is it the point. I'm not "squire" material. I'm not cut out to be part of the "landed gentry". Assuming the impossible. Assuming I'd married and had children. They'd have been brought up *my* way. Not Father's way. Raymond was more Father's type of man.' I smiled wryly. 'The luck of the draw. If Raymond had been the elder son, none of this would have happened.'

134

Softly, slowly and very deliberately, she said, 'And Raymond was prepared to murder you, merely to be able to put "Sir" in front of his name?'

'It was important to him,' I said sadly. 'We all have our own priorities.'

'That's a stupid attitude to take.' She was cross. Very cross. Her eyes blazed and the rhythm of her breathing quickened. 'Excuses! You make excuses for everything. For the inexcusable.'

'Darling, that's not imp–...'

'Of course it's important! He'd *still* do it.'

'Possibly,' I agreed gently. 'Even probably ... given the chance.'

'And you don't *mind?*'

'Of course I mind. I want to live. Now, more than ever. I have you. I have money enough to repair some of the moral damage Father did. I want to live ... now, more than ever.'

'All right.' She nodded her head quickly. 'Don't pay the ransom.'

'Don't ...' My mouth gaped slightly.

'It's easy.' She talked quickly. Breathlessly. 'Let them *have* him. He's not worth a penny, much less half a million. They'll kill him. Of course they will. Kill him, destroy the body. Then ...'

'They might not kill him,' I interrupted.

'Of course they'll kill him. They always do. It's the only way they feel safe. Kill him, hide the body. Destroy it. Anything. Then it's not your fault. You haven't *done* anything. And you're safe. And – honestly – who'll miss him? Who'll mourn?'

'Murder him, by default,' I said softly.

'Oh, my God!' She raised her hands and held them to the side of her head for a moment. '*I don't want you dead.* I don't want that devil Raymond loose, and plotting to ...'

'That's as far as we go.' I held up a hand to silence her. I made the words as stern as I was able. 'I'll not be responsible for any man's death. Not even for you. I'll get the half million

135

ready . . . then we'll wait.'

'What for?'

'For the next move.' I smiled and shook my head slowly. Knowingly. 'Raymond is tamed by this time. Think about it. All the steam *has* to be out of him. Get him free. After that a quiet talk, some involved legal juggling and the cake can be cut into two equal halves. There's enough. More than enough.'

'And the title?'

'I'll renounce it. He'll pick it up. If that's all he wants, there must be a way.'

'And if there isn't?'

'I think we'll have some music.' I pushed myself to my feet and walked to the record shelf. 'They say it soothes the savage breast.'

'I don't want to . . .'

'Oh, yes you do.' I put genuine gentleness into my tone. 'You want to listen to music, my darling, because I refuse to discuss the other thing any more.'

And yet . . .

A man can say he is not greedy. A man can say he lives by certain principles. He can hold all life sacred, cut himself off from the world in order that that world cannot tempt him to alter his life-style, teach himself compassion and a deep love of all things of nature. He can learn to appreciate good music. Read until he has mastered the real difference between good writing and great writing. All these things and more. He can become *civilised*.

The question remains. How deep is that veneer of civilisation, and what does it need to crack it?

Good men – fine men – have slaughtered in the name of patriotism. They have ridden knee-to-knee, and hacked fellow creatures to death for the sake of a banner. They have committed abominations in the cause of an ideal.

As for money – wealth – *great* wealth.

136

Elizabeth had said nothing I myself had not already considered. Considered and not *quite* rejected. To be one of a handful of truly wealthy men. What was that remark Aristotle Onassis once made? 'If you wonder whether or not you can afford a yacht, you can't afford a yacht.' Well, I wasn't interested in yachts, but there was very little I *couldn't* afford. That was the size of the temptation. And (as Elizabeth had indirectly pointed out) so easy. Forget Raymond. Nothing more was needed. I wouldn't have to kill him – not physically kill him: merely allow him to die. No more troubles. No more worries about whether or not he was creeping up to my unprotected back. The young, eccentric baronet who chose to live in a coverted gamekeeper's cottage rather than the big house; who was prepared to use his wealth in the furtherance of *important* things; who was a near-hermit and content to be so.

It was a great temptation, and I could not *quite* make up my mind. I think, sub-consciously, I needed to know the reaction of Raymond before I reached a firm decision.

Next day (the Tuesday) I took him his provisions while Sal trotted happily by my heel. I didn't take the gun. Instinctively, I knew we'd passed the stage where I needed to protect myself. I hadn't tamed him – I had no delusions on that score – but mutual respect, plus the fact that he knew I never carried the key to his shackles, had made for a form of civilised exchange.

I handed him the food and drink and, while he was unpacking the holdall, I took up my favourite position by the fallen birch and lighted a cigarette.

'Bad habits?' He looked and sounded surprised.

'Unfortunately.'

'You're weakening, boy.' He continued to unpack the holdall.

'Not as much as you might wish me to.'

He emptied the holdall and tossed it towards me.

'Yesterday,' I said carefully, 'Father's will was read.'

'Uhu.' He seemed only vaguely interested.

'Step-mother and Elizabeth are taken care of.' I paused, then added, 'After that I get everything . . . you get nothing.'

'So I was told.'

I stared at him.

'By a pipsqueak who works in the solicitor's office.'

'Eric?'

'A big-mouth.' His lips twisted. 'After you told the old man I'd put lead shot into you he changed his will. That's why I'm here . . . isn't it?'

'I'm not sure I know.' I drew on the cigarette. 'Tell me.'

'He changed his will. Left me in the cold. I wanted you out of the way, and I wanted *him* in prison. He wouldn't have lasted three years.'

'He wouldn't have lasted *one* year,' I said sadly. 'We've proof of that already.'

'Better still.' He held out a hand. 'I could use one of those cigarettes.'

I threw him the packet and the matches, and he joined me in smoking before he returned the packet and the box.

'You tried to kill me.' I kept my voice calm and logical. 'That's when this all started.'

He nodded slowly, as if in half-agreement.

'Didn't you?' I pressed.

'I let fly at you.' He moved a hand vaguely. 'Haven't *you* ever wanted to kill somebody who's so damn good? Always so *right*. Always so perfect. Always held up as an example. Always . . .' He drew on the cigarette. 'Anyway, I'd had a lousy day. Missed everything. I even missed you.'

'Was I?' I was surprised.

'What?'

'Held up as an example?'

'Whenever the old bastard wanted to drive the knife home. Whenever he didn't approve of anything.'

'And at other times?'

'You were nothing. Copulation gone wrong.'

'He was that sort of man,' I agreed with a sigh. 'Show him a

138

weak spot. That's where he'd hit you, every time.'

I was, you see, learning things. How wrong I'd been. All this time I'd thought it was the stupid baronetcy he'd been after. But no! The goading. I could understand the goading, and it made more sense. It was the sort of cruelty Father would have enjoyed. On and on and on. The sort of thing capable of driving a hot-tempered man to attempted murder.

'What happens now?' I asked softly.

'You're in the driving seat.'

'I could kill you.'

'No.' He shook his head with absolute assurance. 'You won't kill me, boy. You could have killed me a dozen times, but you haven't. I'll die of old age, but you won't kill me.'

'You stink. You smell. You're filthy,' I observed.

'I've grown used to it.'

'I could just leave you to die. To starve to death.'

'Oh, no.' He chuckled. 'That would be killing me. And you won't.'

I relaxed against the birch and we stared at each other and smoked our cigarettes in silence for all of two minutes.

Then I said, 'We could split it down the middle.'

'The Cutter fortune?'

'There's enough and to spare.'

'And forget this little episode?' There was a touch of harshness in his tone.

'Pay the ransom – pay myself the half million – then release you.'

'Then go half-and-half?'

'Legally. We could have documents drawn up.'

'Easy, eh?' The old Raymond peeped out of his eyes.

'A possible way out.'

'I could let you. I could agree.' The tone hardened. 'I *could* agree . . . and you'd be mug enough to believe me.'

'Meaning you don't agree.'

'Get me out of here, boy. Get me out of this stinking hole.' His voice dropped slightly. 'You'd have half . . . but not for long.'

139

'You'd kill me,' I said sadly.

'Bet every penny you have on it, boy.'

'You've tried twice,' I reminded him.

'You've been *lucky* twice,' he contradicted.

'Or you've been *un*lucky twice.' I drew on the cigarette, then asked, 'Can't we make a pact? Take each other's word?'

'Boy, you're struggling.' He moved his head in mock-sympathy. 'You have a problem. A king-sized problem . . . and no solution.'

Again we smoked in silence for a few moments.

'You *could* give me your word,' I said.

'My word.' It came out with a soft laugh. A rather unpleasant laugh. 'You want my word after all this?'

'I'd accept it.'

'I'll give you my word.' He stabbed the air with the two fingers holding the cigarette. 'The only word that matters. The only promise I'll keep. You've humiliated me, boy. You've abased me. You miserable, twisted bastard. Your mind's as deformed as your body. You've taken a man, and done to him what you wouidn't do to that damn dog of yours. The rats crawl over me at night – did you know that? Rats, ants – God knows what else – trying to get at the food you bring me. They get there sometimes, then *I* have to eat it.' He paused to screw out the cigarette on the planks of the form. 'Something you should remember, boy. One day, when you come, I won't be here. Lesser men than I have broken out of better prisons than this. I'll make it. All day, every day, I have nothing else to do. Just plan. Work out how it can be done. There's a solution, there always is. *Then* I'll keep my promise. The only promise that matters.'

'To murder me,' I breathed.

'The only thing I live for, boy.'

After that, there was no point in discussion. No point in talking. I took him food and drink and, after that visit, I always had the Smith and Wesson handy. A couple of times he tried to enter into some sort of conversation, but I didn't reply. What was the use? The condemned man hasn't much to say to the executioner . . . and we were back to that situaton. His leg was healing; I noted that he could even put some weight on it when he moved from the bed to the bench. From a safe distance I watched the chain and the leg-iron, but saw no signs of weaknesses. He'd escape. He'd certainly try to escape and, given time, it seemed possible. Even probable. And when he *did* escape I could count my own life in days. Possibly hours.

And (dammit!) I couldn't bring myself to kill him or leave him there to die. So, there was only one way left.

Half a million, in used Bank of England notes (fivers and tenners) represents quite a bulk. We used whisky cartons, because they were strongly made and because they were not too heavy to handle. Seven of them, packed solid, then sealed by the bank. No secret markings. No 'bleepers'. Just £500,000 in cold cash.

Gilliant, the chief constable, had raised mild objections.

'My advice is not to pay at first demand.'

'And if he's killed?'

'They won't kill him.'

'Unless you're prepared to give me a written guarantee to that effect . . .'

'Good God, man. You can't expect . . .'

'In other words, you don't know. Like me, you're guessing.'

'All right. Have the bank hold it in readiness.'

'And if they demand it at a moment's notice? In the middle of the night?'

'These people don't work that way.'

'"These people" – as you call them – work any way it pleases them. They also have my brother. I'm not prepared to argue . . . with them or with you.'

'At least let Sergeant Harvey know if they contact you.'

'Of course,' I'd lied.

We'd loaded the cartons into the Polo and I'd driven home and garaged the car. Gilliant had thought I was going to stow as much of the cash as possible in the estate office safe, but Gilliant had been wrong.

I'd arranged with my own bank to have my deposit account – little more than £40,000 – moved over to my current account, then drawn it in cash. I'd given the excuse that I needed ready money with which to pay for major alterations to the cottage. The assistant manager had looked worried ('Any reputable builder will accept a cheque, you know'), but I'd dug in my heels and there wasn't a thing he could do about it.

By Sunday the 12th, the cash side of things was taken care of. I had money enough to live for the rest of my life. *And* in hard currency. No banks. No cheque books. *Ergo*, nothing for the Inland Revenue to latch onto and trace my possible whereabouts.

That afternoon I called at the house and suggested a walk in the forest. Just Elizabeth, Sal and myself.

It was a cold, crisp day. Typical November weather. The ground hard underfoot and, above the leafless branches, a solid gunmetal sky which gave promise of snow in the near future.

We walked slowly, and kept to the recognised paths.

'You love this forest, don't you?' she remarked.

'It's part of my life.' I pointed, 'See that tree, there? Without leaves and from this angle it looks like a prancing horse.'

She nodded her agreement. I wanted her to remember this walk. To *know* it. It was very important that she be able to re-trace the paths we were taking.

'That holly bush. Where the path divides. Huge, isn't it? I think we'll take the right fork.'

Our stroll continued, and I forced her to be interested in our surroundings. The solitary silver birch surrounded by close-cropped grass.

142

'Rabbits play there. That's why the grass is so short. Almost like a lawn.'

And still we walked, and still I made her remember, without knowing she was remembering.

'Round here the path snakes. A double bend . . . there should be a road sign.' I laughed at the non-joke. 'That old oak. See the roots looping out of the soil. You know what they say about the oak?'

'No.'

'For the first hundred years it grows. For the second hundred years it lives. For the third hundred years it dies. That one's an old man.'

'You mean it's dying?'

'It's dying. But we'll both be dead long before *it* is.'

'Do you think . . .' She frowned, then said, 'Do you think Raymond's dead?'

'No.' I made it a one-word answer. I didn't want to tell her unnecessary lies.

'You're going to pay the ransom?'

'Yes.' I pointed. 'That pine. It's one of the tallest trees in this whole forest.'

'He wouldn't do that for you.'

'That pine,' I insisted. 'Look at the shape of it. Look at the height.'

'Oh – er – yes. Magnificent.' Then after a pause. 'If he's still alive, if you pay the ransom and they let him go. He'd have even more reason for killing you.'

I stopped about a hundred yards from the pine. We faced each other, and when I spoke I was sincere, but above all else I wanted her to remember that particular spot.

I said, 'Elizabeth, I love you. There'll never be another woman. I want to kiss you on the lips, but I mustn't. I want to sleep with you – make love to you – but I daren't. Above all else, I want to marry you, but I can't. That's why we're here. At this spot. Our own, secret, magic spot. I can come here. *You* can come here. You can remember this moment for the rest of

143

your life. The tree that looks like a horse. The holly bush where the path divides. The silver birch where the rabbits play. The double bend in the path. That old oak. Then *here*. Where a man – what passes as a man – pledged his heart to you. Wherever we are, whatever people say about me. *Only this is real*.'

I turned and we made our way back the way we'd come. She said little. I think she was stunned at my outburst. But she glanced up at the pine, looked down at the roots of the oak and gently touched the dark green leaves of the holly bush. She knew her way. She'd *always* know her way.

We had tea and cakes at the cottage. Then we talked. Such strange talk. We sat apart, each in our own chair, with Sal resting her chin on the softness of my slipper. And for more than two hours we talked inconsequentialities. We spoke of unimportant things, in short, meaningless sentences. But we both knew. Eah word was a kiss. Each phrase an embrace. We were closer to each other than ever before . . . but so very far apart. When she left I stood at the door and in the half-darkness watched her until she rounded a bend and disappeared from my sight. Heartbroken. Ready to weep. If things went as I planned I'd never see her again.

Harvey called at the cottage next morning. Just after eight o'clock. I'd shaved, dressed and was busy making toast and coffee when he arrived. I invited him to share a snack with me and he seemed happy enough to accept.

When we were seated and eating, he said, 'Nothing from the kidnappers yet?'

'Not yet.' I spread butter and lemon marmalade on the toast. 'They seem to be taking their time.'

'It's the death of your father,' he said.

I chewed and waited for an expansion of this view.

'They're not yet sure who to get in touch with.'

'Possible,' I agreed.

'Maybe a fortnight,' he opined. 'They'll need that to regain their balance.'

'Then . . . me?' I suggested.

'They might drop their price.'

'Really?'

'Father, son. Half-brother, half-brother. There isn't quite the close tie.'

'A sort of Dutch auction,' I smiled.

'Y'see.' He bit into the toast and talked as he chewed. 'We have to be very objective. Put ourselves in their shoes. The death of your father . . . something they hadn't counted on. An alteration to their plans. They're professionals, of course.'

'Of course.'

'They'll have planned everything down to the last detail.'

'Of course,' I repeated.

'A thing like this happens, they'll need to adjust their plans.'

'Naturally.'

'I mean . . .' He warmed to his theme. 'They don't know – they don't know for *certain* – that your father showed that original note to *anybody*. In that case – if they reach *that* conclusion – they're back at the beginning. Another note. This time addressed to you.'

'What of Raymond?' I asked with some interest.

'Sir?'

'He hasn't been around lately. He wasn't at the cremation, that's one thing they *do* know.'

'Ah!'

'Yes?'

'Does he – er – go off on his own sometimes?'

'Sometimes.'

'In that case . . .'

'But he'd come back for his father's funeral.'

'Ah, yes. Of course.' He took another bite of toast. 'But that's something else they don't know. Not for *certain*. They'll be edgy. Very edgy.'

'He could, of course, be dead,' I murmured.

'We don't work on that assumption, sir. We don't . . .'

'In which case, they wouldn't be at all edgy.'

145

'If they've committed murder they'll . . .'

'Quite. But who are "they"? The whole stupid arrangement has blown up in their faces. They do away with Raymond, dispose of the body, and by this time they're well hidden in the tall timber. A fair question, sergeant. Who the hell are you looking for? How many? All men or both sexes? Black or white? And where?'

'We like to be optimistic, sir.'

'Do you?' I stared at him, swallowed my last piece of toast and reached for my cigarettes. 'Tell me, sergeant, how many crimes has optimism solved?'

'I'm sorry, sir.' He looked crestfallen. 'I sound like a fool.'

'You're not a fool, Sergeant.' I lighted the cigarette, then quietly, sombrely, said, 'You just haven't yet learned to think like a criminal.'

He left shortly afterwards, and I have no doubt my remark puzzled him. But *I* knew what I meant. *I* knew how criminals thought . . . if, that is, they all thought like me. They felt guilty. Guilty as the very devil. And scared. Terrified. Never mind the excuses – the so-called 'extenuating circumstances' – they didn't mean a thing. The hatred had gone, and so had the self-congratulatory feeling of having out-witted Raymond. There was no room for anything other than the massive fusion of guilt and fear. That and misery. Abject misery. Misery so great that I truly wished I had not jumped to one side when Raymond had first squeezed the trigger of that shot-gun.

I was a most unhappy man, but I knew I had one final task to perform before I ran for it.

Strangely, the solicitor raised no objections at all. I explained that I had decided to take a prolonged holiday. Nowhere in particular, just away from it all. He agreed that that was what I needed. I asked that Elizabeth's signature on any document, cheque, etc., should carry the same weight as my own and, while I waited, he had a typist draft out the necessary authorisation. I signed it, it was witnessed, we shook hands and he wished me bon voyage.

As simple as that.

Having loaded the Polo, I took Sal for a last walk in our beloved woods. Not a long walk. Just a quick, sad 'goodbye', then she clambered onto the front passenger seat and we were away.

I called at a local garage and had the tank filled with petrol. The attendant knew me. Eventually, they'd ask him questions, and he'd tell them I was heading south. I was, until I joined the A170, then I turned east. I hit the coast road at about dusk, turned right and booked in at an hotel on the outskirts of Bridlington. I gave my name as Deverell . . . and that's been my name ever since. David Deverell.

Next morning I drove into Bridlington, left Sal in the car and walked around the town. I walked slowly, in order to hide my slight limp. I called into Woolworths and bought a small notebook, then I went to three of the main high street banks and opened an account in each. £2,000 each time: 'David Deverell' but each with a different address which I'd noted in my book. £2,000 in four of the major building societies; again 'Deverell' and, again, four different addresses. That was £14,000 safe and get-at-able, and all before lunch.

In the afternoon I drove north to Scarborough. Again, four building societies – different ones – and £2,000 in paid-up shares in each. 'David Deverell' and with different addresses noted from streets and roads I'd passed in the town. £22,000 slopping about, and already lost among the millions of legitimate cash handled by these people. I bought new number plates for the Polo, and was amazed to discover the ease with which number plates *can* be bought; any number you care to come up with and stamped out while you wait.

I still counted myself 'safe', but gave myself only one more day in which to be able to wander around at will. I needed a disguise. I'd already decided to let my whiskers grow into a beard, but my shortened leg posed a problem. Why not accentuate it? It seemed an excellent idea. I called at a surgical outfitters and bought elbow crutches, cotton wool and crepe bandages, then I returned to the car. I removed my built-up boot, rolled up my trouser leg, then padded my foot and lower leg with cotton wool. Then, crepe bandages until the foot was twice its normal size. I rolled down the trouser leg, eased myself from the car and adjusted the crutches. Easy! I was obviously a man recovering from a serious foot or leg injury, who had to walk with the help of crutches while he kept his injured leg bent and the foot clear of the ground. Short of using a tape measure, nobody could have guessed that the 'injured' leg was more than two inches shorter than the other. Nor was it difficult to get the hang of using the elbow crutches. Indeed, polite people stood aside to let me pass.

Sal gave every indication of being both puzzled and displeased. She was puzzled at the antics of her master who, for no known canine reason, shuffled along at a snail's pace, hampered by two lengths of metal. She was displeased at having to spend so much time alone in the car. But her real displeasure centred upon the indignity of having to wear a collar and lead. She accepted it, but with bad grace. I think her resentment stemmed from the implied suggestion that she might leave my heel without permission. Crazy, to talk about a dog like that? Not if you've really owned a dog . . . or, perhaps, if a dog has ever owned *you*. And certainly not with a dog like Sal. She was a perfect lady; good tempered and polite. But, while still wagging her stump of a tail, she could convey her feeling of outrage.

Looking back, I cannot remember once giving thought to Raymond. I had my plans worked out and they were going beautifully and, if things continued to go well, he'd be free to bath, shave, eat and drink very shortly. Three days (thereabouts) without food and water would do him no real harm. Furthermore, I had more important things to think about.

That evening (Tuesday, November 14th) I drove south to Filey. There was an inn; a comfortable enough place, where they allowed me to have Sal in the bedroom with me. I stayed there the night.

That was where I wrote the letter.

Elizabeth my darling,

This is the most difficult letter I have ever had to write, but write it I must. We shall never see each other again, and that is punishment enough for my cowardice. I ask one final favour of you. Go to our spot in the forest. Our own magic spot. Take the enclosed key with you. When you reach the spot where I gave you my love leave the path. Walk west for a good half mile. Keep walking west, and call Raymond's name. In time he will answer you. Find him and use the key to free him.

I think I need say no more, other than that I will always love you,

Lionel

I placed the letter and the key to the leg-iron in a stiff brown envelope addressed to Elizabeth, then tucked the envelope into the inside pocket of my jacket, and even then I gave no thought to Raymond. All my thoughts were centred upon Elizabeth.

The next morning I was up early, had a quick breakfast and was away. The A165, all the way to Kingston-upon-Hull, then over the Humber Bridge and east to Cleethorpes. I pushed the Polo as hard as I dare. It was November and out of season, but the days were short and the there-and-back journey was not a joy ride. Fast, therefore, but always remembering that an accident would reveal a king's ransom in used notes in the boot and rear seat of the car.

I ate a late lunch at a café, bought Sal a pork pie to sustain her, then let her run around on the sands for a good half hour. I felt a little like apologising for the pork pie, and I had something of a problem convincing the restaurant people that dogs need a drink of water occasionally. For that reason, I gave her the freedom of the sands when, in fact, I would have liked to have been on my way back.

149

I posted the letter and the key to Elizabeth. I used a second class stamp; postal delivery being what it is, that gave me an extra day at least. Then we were on our way north again.

We hit the fog at a little village called Fraisthorpe, south of Bridlington. What the locals call a 'sea fret'; damp and thick and it was already dark. The sort of conditions through which only fools drive unless they have urgent business. I pulled into a lay-by, switched off the lights, wound up the windows, locked the doors and tipped my seat to its lay-back position.

Cat-napping was all I could manage. It was too cold for comfort, and at about two in the morning the thought struck me that I was very vulnerable. All the yobs weren't in the big cities, and the wrong people caught out in this lot might not think twice about hi-jacking a parked car. I leaned back, opened a suitcase, took out the Smith and Wesson and slipped it under the driving seat. I had too much to lose to take chances.

Dawn came, and with the light a slight thinning of the mist. I returned the driving seat to an upright position then, with Sal, stepped from the car to empty my bladder, while Sal did likewise. It was a cold, grey, damp world. A closed-in world, with the webs of spiders, sketched out in tiny droplets, linking the leafless branches of the hedgerow. Gossamer lace holding fairy pearls. And silence. Not the silence of my forest, but an icy, blanketing silence which, somehow, was threatening.

We returned to the car, I switched on the lights and started the engine, and in careful third gear we continued north. Past Bridlington, past Reighton, past Filey, then just north of Gristhorpe I saw the caravan park through the thinning mist. It was out of season – well out of season – but it was one of those caravan set-ups which, even at the height of summer, look what they are. Cheap-jack and run on a shoe-string. That was fine by me. That was the sort of place I wanted.

I drew in and a man wearing patched trousers, braces and a collarless shirt approached me. He was, he explained, the 'caretaker'. The 'manager' didn't live on the site; he lived somewhere Manchester way. Could he be contacted? No, he wouldn't like it. The site was closed for winter. Couldn't just one caravan be let?

I pointed to one of the caravans which stood slightly apart from the rest. 'That one, for example?'

'No. The electricity was switched off more than a month back.'

'Couldn't it be switched on again?'

'You don't know the gaffer. He'd know. He'd count the units.'

'All right,' I pleaded. 'No electricity. An oil lamp is all I need. An oil lamp, a Calor Gas fire.' I glanced down at my bandaged foot. 'I need rest and quiet for a few weeks. I'm prepared to pay high-season rates. I'll be no trouble. You won't even know I'm here.'

'He wouldn't like it.' There was indecision in the man's tone.

'Cash,' I added meaningfully.

'I – er . . .'

'That van.' I pointed. 'Just open it up Clean sheets each week until I find somewhere permanent. That's all I'm asking. Cash, and no receipts asked for.'

He rubbed his unshaven jowl and pondered, 'He'll not be around this side of Christmas.'

'I'll be away before then.'

He nodded slowly. 'Don't bother about the gas. There's a bottle nearly full outside one of the other vans. I'll switch 'em. But I can't fix the electricity.'

'Thanks.' I opened my wallet, peeled out five ten-pound notes and handed them to him through the open car window. 'Let me know when I owe you more.'

He was a petty scoundrel. Of course he was. His name, I discovered, was Tommy, and I have no doubt that the unknown 'gaffer' paid him as little as possible. Equally, I have no doubt that the type of family using that class of caravan site forever found fault. But Tommy could cope. Tommy knew all the tricks, and Tommy also knew when he was onto a good thing. As with me. Fifty pounds a week for the loan of a caravan key, plus the mild inconvenience of taking the bed linen to some local launderette once a week. Money for old rope, and he appreciated it. He delivered *The Yorkshire Post* to me every day. He even supplied two paraffin pressure lamps, and a steady supply of fuel to give me no need for an electricity link-up. The gas cylinder fed both a tiny fire and a miniature cooker, therefore I had warmth and the wherewithal to knock up a scratch meal if needs be.

I also had a base, and *The Yorkshire Post* provided me with news of what might be happening at the Cutter household.

I started my search that same afternoon. The mist had lifted and I left the site, called at Scarborough, opened paid-up share accounts with two more building societies, then drove inland from the sea. I kept to unclassified roads, and passed villages I'd never heard of before. Hackness and Langdale End, Sawdon and Hutton Buscel. I was north of the Wolds, and in the Carrs. Wild country, much of it forest country east of Pickering. I saw the sort of place I was after more than once, but always occupied, with never a hint that it might soon become vacant.

The Friday, too. This time I drove nearer to the Wolds. Fordon on to Wold Newton, on to Thwing, on to Grinsdale. Narrow roads with off-shoots unmarked on any road map. I took these off-shoots, too, but they led nowhere or, at best, to some isolated farmstead. I ate at inns when the mood took me. I stopped the car often and wandered around a countryside which, although new to me, I knew I could grow to love. The same Saturday, the same Sunday. Every inch of countryside north of Beverley for twenty miles or so from the coast. With Sal as a willing, almost eager, companion. She had new scents to excite her every day. New verges along which to sniff. She enjoyed herself. Me? I wasn't yet worried, but I was starting to wonder *when*?

My problem, on the face of it, seemed a foolish problem. The money. There is a limit to the number of building societies. There is a limit to the amount of cash which can be passed over

152

the counter of a building society, or for that matter a bank, without arousing at least mild curiosity. I was becoming aware that half a million pounds in Bank of England notes is an almost embarrassingly large amount of money. The 'placing' of it was far more difficult than I had imagined.

There was also the business of the bumpf which every society and every bank automatically sends off to a new customer. God only knew how many would be returned with 'Not at this address' scrawled across the envelope and this, too, might lead to questions and, eventually, trouble.

That Sunday evening, in the warmth of the caravan, I thought and re-thought the problem. I reached certain tentative conclusions; that to withdraw money, in cheque form, from the building societies and transfer the cheques to my bank accounts seemed a first and obvious step. Thereafter, to have a word with Tommy and arrange for my mail to be forwarded to *his* address. More work, more worry, more signatures of 'D. Deverell'. This business of removing oneself from the face of the earth was not as simple as it had at first seemed.

I was restless all that night. When I did sleep, I had bad dreams. Elizabeth, Sal, Raymond and Father were all chasing me. I zig-zagged, but they always cut me off and, when they caught up with me, something very terrible was going to happen. I didn't know what. Just . . . something.

I awoke with the dawn, and as I was brewing tea, Tommy opened the door of the van and tossed in *The Yorkshire Post*. I poured the tea, picked up the newspaper and opened it.

The headlines . . .

BARONET GIVES LIFE FOR YOUNGER BROTHER'S FREEDOM

Then, in lesser headlines . . .

SIR LIONEL CUTTER MURDERED

Then came the 'story' . . .

It can now be revealed that the younger son of the late Sir Lionel Cutter was recently kidnapped from his home . . . an undisclosed ransom . . . the police believe the kidnappers contacted the present Sir Lionel Cutter . . . took the agreed sum to a pre-arranged meeting place . . . apparently insisted upon seeing his brother, Raymond, before handing over the money . . . an outhouse at an isolated farmstead . . . Sir Lionel tried to pull the mask from one of the criminals . . . was shot in the chest at close quarters and killed outright by two shots from a sawn-off shotgun . . . brother, Raymond, was bundled into a car after being blindfolded . . . a long journey, before being thrown from the car . . . a telephone kiosk, from where he called the police.

It made no sense. No sense at all. A pack of lies which, in effect, made me a dead man. I re-read the whole piece. More slowly this time. Then, as the possibilities and the probabilities slipped into place, it *began* to make sense.

Elizabeth! I could visualise her standing there, with the key in her hand demanding terms. She'd know I was on the run. She'd know the police would hunt until they found me. A bargain, then. Freedom, in exchange for this pack of lies. It would slam the door in the face of the police. They'd still search, but they'd be searching for a non-existent outhouse and they'd be searching for a non-existent corpse.

Raymond? He'd become *Sir* Raymond Cutter. The Cutter fortune would be *his*. He had everything to gain and nothing to lose by accepting the terms.

Oh yes, there was sense there all right. The perfect confidence trick. Freedom for Raymond . . . but, equally, freedom for me.

As the saying goes, 'Love will find a way'. It had done this time, too.

The pressure was off and, with something of a shock, I realised how great the pressure had been. I was able to take my time; I used three full days in which to perform fiscal gymnastics until all the cash was out of building societies and safely deposited in the 'big four' high street banks.

I still scanned *The Yorkshire Post* with some eagerness. The police were making their usual noises of official optimism. On the Wednesday there was a photograph of Elizabeth and a slightly po-faced statement from the solicitor saying that she was leaving for a prolonged holiday in the sunshine, destination a secret, pending the quietening of the initial enquiry. Clever girl! It removed her from centre-stage and left Raymond to think up answers to possible awkward questions. He'd committed himself too far to retract what he'd already said. He was holding the baby, and if it needed a nappy-change that was his worry, too.

I could, of course, by this time write cheques. Equally (and very often) I could make minor purchases with banknotes, pocket the change, and when the weight of coins had become ridiculous, call into some strange bank on my travels and change the coins into other banknotes. It was devious. It was going to take forever. But that was okay. Thanks to Elizabeth I *had* 'forever'. Eventually the 'ransom money' would be circulating nicely, 'David Deverell' would have four perfectly legal and very healthy bank accounts and, when that moment arrived, a completely new personality would have been created.

By the end of November I had discarded the elbow crutches, re-donned my built-up shoe, and with the aid of a walking stick and by stepping carefully, could mask my infirmity even from Tommy.

And still I searched for a new home.

I found the place on Saturday, December the 2nd. Tucked away in the Cleveland Hills, five miles past the village of Farndale East and hidden up a branch valley from Bransdale.

The road had petered out and I'd parked and locked the Polo and was taking Sal for a walk in the frost-nipped air.

Then I saw the smoke. A thin spiral which eased its way skywards from behind a shoulder of hillside. I explored . . . and there it was. Centuries old, with thick stone walls and a stone-paved roof. Uncared for but (to me) beckoning and silently pleading to be loved. There was a black car outside and a group of solemn-faced men engaged in some sort of discussion. Very tentatively, I approached them.

A portly man, dressed in dark clothes, spotted me and came to meet me.

'Are you Mr Evans?' he asked quietly.

'No. My name's Deverell.'

'A relative, perhaps?'

'Relative?' A slightly embarrassing realisation began to dawn.

'We're waiting for Mr Evans, his nephew.'

'His – er – nephew?'

'The deceased.'

'Oh!'

'Ah!' The portly man glanced over my shoulder and said, 'This will be him.' I turned and saw a red Cortina feeling its way cautiously towards us along the dirt road.

Thereafter, I was ill-mannered to a degree. I openly admit it, but the ancient, isolated cottage held me spellbound, and although I stayed at a discreet distance, with Sal sitting quietly by my heel, I didn't leave. Nor did it seem particularly indelicate on my part. The man from the Cortina was middle-aged and looked cheerful enough. He certainly did not give the appearance of somebody recently bereaved.

The four men went inside the cottage and I waited. They were in there for the best part of an hour, and when they came out, the man from the Cortina shook hands all round and made for his car.

It was now or never.

I walked forward and said, 'Er – Mr Evans.'

156

'Yes?' He stopped, turned and smiled.

'It's – er . . .' I felt myself blush as I continued, 'I understand somebody has died.'

'My uncle.' The smile came and went. 'Ninety-four. He's had a good innings. Did you know him?'

'Er – no – I'm afraid not.'

'No. He kept himself very much to himself. The undertaker . . .' He moved his head, indicating the portly man. 'He had the devil's own job tracing me. Next-of-kin. Even *I* didn't know where he lived. Not exactly. Up here in the hills . . . as vague as that.'

He paused, and waited for me to say something.

'The – er – house?' I said awkwardly. 'The cottage?'

'Who'll want to buy *that*?' he sighed. 'Out here. Miles from . . .'

'I'll buy it,' I blurted.

He frowned puzzlement.

'Look.' I moved my hands a little wildly. 'I'm – I'm not a ghoul . . . anything like that. I – I know it sounds like it, but it isn't that way at all. Pure coincidence. My solemn word, pure coincidence. That's my car. You must have passed it, down the road. The Polo. I was – y'know – just stretching my legs, taking my dog for a walk and I saw it. The cottage, I mean. I've been looking for something like that – *exactly* like that – for weeks. Isolated. Miles from anywhere.' On an impulse, I added, 'I'm a naturalist. For me it's ideal.'

'For weekends?'

'To *live* in,' I assured him.

'I – I think your wife should . . .'

'I'm not married,' I interrupted. 'Just me. It's what I want.'

He took cigarettes from his pocket and offered me one. When we'd lighted them, he said, 'Let's go to the car. Talk this thing over.'

In the Cortina, he said, 'You say you're a naturalist?'

'Yes.'

'What's your name?'

'Deverell. David Deverell.'

'I can't say I've ever heard of you.'

'Amateur,' I assured him. 'I haven't written books, given lectures, appeared on TV – anything like that. It's a hobby . . . an obsession, really.'

'Equally,' he said slowly and with disarming honesty, 'you could be some city smart boy out for a bargain.'

'No!' I had to convince him. I *had* to have that cottage. 'Look . . . name the price. Have it valued, if that's the way you want to do it. Anything reasonable – anything not too outrageous – I won't quibble. I'm fortunate. I'm alone in the world. I had a rich father. I don't have to mess about with mortgages.'

'You're in something of a hurry,' he remarked. 'Unless I'm mistaken, you haven't yet seen inside the place.'

'It's *where* I want to be,' I pleaded.

'All right.' He nodded half-satisfaction. 'But there's the furniture. Some of it's old. It might be valuable. I don't know much about these things.'

'Nor I.'

'That's what you *say*.'

'I don't want the furniture,' I assured him. 'Take it to a saleroom. Sell it that way. Or if you want to have a valuer out, that's fine by me. Get it valued. I'll pay. What I don't want *I'll* sell.'

'Mr Deverell,' he said, 'You don't *buy* houses that way.'

'You do.' I put all the urgency of which I was capable into my voice. 'You see something you want. Something unique. Some once-in-a-lifetime thing you know you'll never be able to buy again. If you have the money – if you can afford it – that's *just* how you buy it. Anything! Otherwise, you might live the rest of your life with regrets.'

He stared at me, then chuckled quietly and said, 'You're a lucky man, Deverell.'

'Only if you allow me to be lucky.'

He opened the car door, and said, 'You'd better see inside the cottage. Then, if you feel the same way, we'll call in at a

158

decent restaurant, and go over the final details while we eat.'

It is hard to believe (indeed, as I write this outline of what happened so few years ago, it is hard for *me* to believe) but it is perfectly true. Christmas 1978 passed and 1978 moved into 1979 without me being really aware of those dates.

Of course I bought the cottage, and the acre of land that went with it. I probably paid £1,000 more than it was worth, but what matter? I paid for it being stripped of furniture and for that furniture to be taken to a saleroom at Whitby, but, again, what matter? By mid-December I was installed in a two-berth caravan, parked alongside the cottage and, while the solicitors were performing their conveyancing contortions, I was already making the place *my* place.

My first realisation was that the Polo was unsuitable. I used it to drag the caravan into position and that of itself, once we'd left the tarmac road surface, almost ruined a perfectly good car. One night I drove it south-east, parked on the edge of a picnic site between Langdale End and Harwood Dale, then, in the small hours, removed the petrol cap, ran a trail of petrol for about fifty yards and dropped a lighted match. The tank blew up and, with it, a first-class car. I was alone and, long before officialdom arrived, I was hobbling my way towards Burniston and, a few hours after dawn, I telephoned a taxi firm and was driven to Scarborough. It was (I realised then, and realise now) a calculated risk. A blown up car followed, a few hours later, by a taxi ride to Scarborough. Given time, the police would connect the two, but given *time*. Time and destinations were the two things I juggled with. I had a meal in Scarborough, then caught one of the regular service buses to Bridlington. There I strolled around until I saw what I was after. A moderately-priced, second-hand Ford van standing for sale on a garage forecourt. I haggled a little, took it for a test drive, then bought it. With it came a Registration Document, and my own Certificate of Insurance covered my purchase and driving of it.

159

The Certificate of Insurance was a new one, made out to 'David Deverell' of my newly purchased home. I was therefore documenting the new character I'd assumed a little more. I was gradually proving possible what a lot of people might have thought *im*possible. I was *becoming* 'David Deverell'.

From then on, it was work.

Because of where it was the cottage had electricity, but that's all it had. It had a septic tank. It had its own hundred-foot-deep bore-hole which delivered pure, ice-cold water. A large downstairs room and a not-too-small kitchen. Open stairs which led to two bedrooms. The whole surrounded by an acre of uncultivated garden.

The first job was to get down to basics. To strip.

I drove to Scarborough and spent money at a good do-it-yourself store. Chisels, hammers, wire-brushes, rippers and sacks. Then I started. Carefully, slowly, I took every square inch of plaster from the walls, downstairs and upstairs. I pulled down the plaster-boards from the ceilings and exposed the good oak of the joists and rafters, and the underside of the upstairs rooms. No frippery. I wanted nothing hidden. I loaded the rubble into sacks, loaded the sacks into the van and dumped their contents at an official council tip some fifteen miles away.

When I was down to good Yorkshire stone, I wire-brushed it to rid it of all dust and loose pieces. Every room. Every corner. Then I bought trowels, sharp sand and good cement and carefully, patiently, re-pointed every gap between every stone. I went a little mad. Nothing was too good. Nothing was good *enough*. I took every flake of paint from the skirting boards; sanded and scraped until my fingers were raw; fitted sealed-unit double-glazing, then fixed a sloping tiled outer sill and a two-inch-thick seasoned oak inner sill; brought the window openings in to meet the new fixtures, filled in and allowed to set, filled in and allowed to set, time and time again until I knew nothing could shift those windows, and until I knew not a single draught could find its way into the house. I bought an extension ladder and, risking my neck, repeated the same process on the underside of the flagged roof, between the flags and the stays and between the flags and the rafters. Then more sanding, more scraping, more pointing.

At some time during this period the old year went and the new year arrived. At some time during this same period I became the legal owner of the property. I took time off to drive to the solicitor's office, sign papers and hand over a cheque for the conveyancing. Other than that, my only relaxation was in taking Sal for a five mile walk across a countryside which was becoming harder and bleaker as the true winter increased its grip.

I felt no cold. Had it been mid-summer I would have felt no heat. At times I was caught outdoors without appropriate outer clothes in a downpour or a sudden blizzard. I felt nothing. Only the cottage mattered. In some extraordinary way, we were one. The cottage was part of me, and I was part of the cottage. We were a world. *The* world. The only real world.

I'd run wire from the cottage to the caravan, and a single light bulb and a one-bar electric fire provided me with all the comfort I needed. I awoke at dawn and worked until the daylight failed. I lived on scratch meals; scratch meals, mugs of tea and cigarettes.

My beard and hair had grown long and bedraggled. The immersion heater in the cylinder gave enough hot water for me to sluice myself down towards the end of each day.

I remember the date. I remember it quite clearly. It was a Sunday – February the 25th, 1979 – and in that late afternoon, as the daylight thinned and the gloom of the early evening strengthened, I realised that the 'change of direction' point had been reached. I'd stripped everything needing to be stripped; gutted the cottage's interior to its bare bones. Now the 'creating' part had to begin.

161

The creation (and, I emphasise, *creation*, not *re*-creation) lasted until July. It would be tedious to go into fine details. Suffice to say that I bought books in order to learn things; that I re-wired the whole cottage; that the inner faces of the walls and the underside slope of the roof carried three coats of size, two coats of primer and three coats of dull gloss ivory coloured paint; that every inch of woodwork had been lovingly stained and darkened, then varnished; that the living room and the single large bedroom boasted top-quality carpet tiles of a deep claret.

No gimmicks. No cut corners. I had book-shelves galore; all of seasoned oak and all carefully fitted. I had music; a hi-fi, stereo music centre – one of the best on the market – with twin double-speakers fitted at an angle high at opposite corners of the lounge and sending their respective sound down towards the wing-chair I favoured. I bought furniture, piece at a time. Good stuff. Craftsman-made to last a lifetime.

The bathroom was floored in cork tiles. The kitchen in ceramic tiles. Stand-lamps and table lamps gave light, and six (two pairs) of low-wattage, orange-shaded lamps hanging from the beams gave a warm glow when darkness came. The real warmth, however, came from the open fire, with its fire-basket and carefully regulated draught, while background heat was provided by slim, night-storage heaters strategically placed along the walls; capable of being regulated and (as it turned out) killing the morning chill when I climbed from bed in winter.

God, how I loved that cottage! And still love it.

I re-stocked my library and record collection, then added to it. I lost count of the books I bought, but I read, and often re-read, every one of them. None were there for show. In an idle moment (and they came rarely!) I once estimated that I had music – *good* music – at my finger-tips to last me for more than a week, non-stop, night and day.

Television?

Never! I wanted no 'window on the world'. I had my world; a world peopled by myself and Sal. I had a world beyond my door. A wild and untamed world ever ready to be explored and always capable of springing pleasant surprises.

Above all, I had peace.

Over that summer of 1979, I applied for a Provisional Driving Licence, passed the driving test and obtained a valid driving licence in the name of David Deverell. I rid myself of the caravan and the Ford; I traded them both in in part-exchange for a nearly-new Land Rover. The Ford had done valiant work, the caravan had served its purpose and I knew what the path beyond the tarmac road was like in mid-winter. I needed a strong, four-wheel-drive vehicle if I was not to be captive for anything up to three months of the year.

I replaced my wardrobe. Stout clothes, without frippery. I had my hair cut and my beard trimmed.

In short, I quietened down. The dynamo which had driven me for so long steadied, and I caught up with months of lost sleep. It was a lazy summer, and I was as happy as I think I'd ever been.

I bought and installed a deep-freeze.

I bought a good rotovator and tackled the garden surrounding the cottage. At some moment, or perhaps it was a gradual realisation, the thought struck me that I was . . . not exactly *lonely*, but very alone. I had Sal, of course – I had my music, my books, my walks in the country and now the problem of the garden – but nobody was there to *speak* to me. I lacked conversation. My brain was becoming ossified. I was starting to hold conversations with myself. Even arguments with myself.

It began to worry me, but there was no obvious answer. I was not of a social disposition and never had been. What few friends I'd ever had had become friends very gradually and without conscious effort on my part. My present neighbours I knew, but only by sight. A handful of hill-farmers who nodded silent greeting if we happened to pass. No word. Just the nod. A silent breed; silent almost to the point of being surly. Like me.

Their own business was their only concern. I didn't know their names. I have no doubt they didn't know mine. I was a 'comer-in'. A 'foreigner'. But I wasn't nosey, and I wasn't pushing, therefore they tended to accept me.

Nevertheless, there were times when I felt very much alone. My need was conversation. Not chatter. Not gossip. Just quiet talk with, perhaps, friendly disagreement. Like I'd once had with Elizabeth.

Dear, sweet Elizabeth. God, how I missed her. For weeks – for months – I'd been too busy to think of anything other than the work in hand. I'd flogged myself to a standstill, and had had no time to concentrate upon anything other than the work in hand. But now that work was as near completion as it would ever be, and I had time to think. But empty thoughts. Unvoiced thoughts. Thoughts which lacked a sounding board from which they might rebound and, in so doing, expand and lead to other avenues of thoughts.

Then in October – it was a Saturday, October the 6th, 1979 – I met the schoolmaster.

I know little of art. Even today, I know little of art, but on that Saturday afternoon, I knew even less. Yet even the ignorant are, albeit unconsciously, aware of certain things. Certain differences. Light, for example. Had you asked, even in those days, I would have explained, with some awkwardness perhaps, that at (say) 2 p.m. on a cloudless day, the sunlight of mid-July differs from the sunlight of early October. The difference, to put it crudely, is the difference between gold and silver. Perhaps the heat has something to do with it. Perhaps nature's awareness of the nearness of coming winter. For whatever reason, the colouring in the latter part of the year seems crisper and, in some subtle way, less brash. Of necessity, harder to capture on canvas.

Had you asked, on that October Saturday afternoon, I might have made some awkward attempt at explaining the difference, but it would have been a poor and stumbling effort.

At that time, the only thing I knew was the different 'feel'. I recognised the difference, but not with my eyes.

We'd wandered a little off the usual paths, and Sal was enjoying herself scampering among the heather then, quite suddenly, I saw the parked car, and alongside the car the man with easel and brushes.

He was a middle-aged man; a few years older than myself. He was prematurely bald, except for a fringe of grey-white hair at the back and sides. Not particularly heavily built, but portly enough to look a shade ridiculous on the canvas-seated collapsible stool upon which he was perched. His concentration was complete. He neither saw nor heard either Sal or myself. I called Sal to heel and slowly, gently – almost on tip-toe – we moved nearer.

Strange, in retrospect – looking back almost four years – that I *went* to this man. That I was drawn to him. The easel, perhaps? Set up an easel, produce paints and brushes and, like a magnet, strangers are drawn towards you. To see. To watch. Not to make a nuisance of themselves. Merely, perhaps, to feel they are *there* at the birth of what might become a masterpiece. That may have been part of it – I make no claim to be different from other men – but there was something else. Something which made me overcome my natural shyness. Something between this concentrating man and myself.

He was working in oils. Occasionally, he took a palette knife from the box which was upturned alongside him and which he used as a makeshift table, but in the main it was brush-work. A capturing of the contours and a freezing of the shifting colours. Twice he placed his brush on the box, took pad and charcoal and sketched some detail . . . presumably to be added later.

For all of twenty minutes I watched without him noticing me. Then he sighed, placed brush and palette on the box and tapped the pockets of his stained jacket.

'A cigarette?' I held an opened packet towards him.

165

'Ah!' He became aware of my presence with something of a start and, for a moment, I thought I saw something not far from fright in his eyes.

'I'm sorry,' I apologised. 'I was curious.'

'That's . . .' He waved a hand. 'That's quite all right.' He took a cigarette, and when we'd both lighted our cigarettes, a timid smile lighted his face, and he said, 'Thank you.'

'I shouldn't have startled you,' I said.

'I'm easily startled.' The gentle smile remained. 'I concentrate too much.'

'You – er . . .' I nodded towards the canvas. 'You have great skill.'

'Not enough.' He sighed. 'Enough to know I may one day be good, but I'll never be great.'

'Enough?' I raised an eyebrow.

'I'm past the learner's class.' I liked his complete lack of false modesty. 'I know what's good. I even know *I* can be good, given the right mood and the right landscape. But never *great*. Like music.'

'I know nothing of art.' I lowered myself onto the rough turf alongside him. 'But I know a little about music.'

'You play?'

'No. But I listen . . . and can appreciate.'

'Then you know.' He spread his hands. 'The good and the great. There's a chasm. Only genius can bridge it. Not knowledge, not practice, not application . . . genius.'

'You live near here?' I asked timidly.

'Leeds.'

'Oh?'

'I'm a schoolmaster. Assistant head of a comprehensive. My wife died recently . . .'

'I'm sorry.'

'I'm not.' There was no bitterness. Only simple truth. 'She'd suffered far too long.' He paused, stared with out-of-focus eyes into the distance, then continued, 'We're told prolonged pain is a purifying experience. It isn't, despite what the clerics claim.

166

It's ugly, and in time it turns the sufferer ugly. Not physically ugly. Just . . . beyond reason. She asks "Why?" Why *her*? She's done no real wrong – lived a good life – so why *her*? And there's no answer. No comfort. Nothing you can say that makes sense. You're helpless, and you wish it would end. And when it does . . .' He looked at me and shook his head, sadly. 'You should cry. People expect you to cry. But you *can't*. The relief – the relief for her and for yourself – is bigger than the sadness. They think you don't *feel*. They think you didn't love her. Don't miss her.' He screwed out the cigarette then softly, savagely, ended, 'The bloody fools!'

The impression was that he'd found a stranger to whom he could open his heart, and I was glad. There was about him an honesty which was immediately apparent. He picked up a brush and idly – as to find work for his hand – touched the unfinished painting. It added nothing, altered nothing. It was a gesture. The gesture of a man who (perhaps) hoped he hadn't made a mistake.

I remained silent for a few minutes, finished my own cigarette, then pushed myself to my feet.

'You're staying somewhere?' I asked.

'A pub at Helmsley.'

'You'll pass my place on the way back. Before you hit the road proper. A cottage on the left.'

'I think I know it.'

'Call in,' I invited. 'Trout. Do you like trout?'

'Yes, but . . .'

'Nothing fancy. Just in butter. I'll have it ready. We can listen to good music and talk.'

I left before he could answer. I willed him to call. He was what I needed. A companion – *one* companion – as much in need of a friend as I was.

The truth is, it had taken no small amount of courage on my part. To invite a complete stranger to my table, but not for a moment did I ever regret it. Companionship has to start somewhere. That was where ours started. That trout dinner. We talked music, we talked art, we talked books.

'I've often wondered why *Tono Bungay* is regularly made required reading for English Lit. exams.'

'It's a good book. Wells is a fine writer.'

'Probably, but it's not his best work. And it's not for young minds. At times it's a little like wading through literary treacle.'

'What then?'

'Something they can get *interested* in. Something *encouraging*. To show them that reading is a pleasure . . . not a boring necessity.'

'Such as what?'

'Buchan. *The Thirty-Nine Steps. Greenmantle.*'

'Thrillers?' I smiled at the thought.

'My dear David, Buchan's writing equalled that of Wells. He wrote beautiful prose . . . that it took the form of adventure stories is neither here nor there. The kids would enjoy it, and at the same time *learn*.'

Then as his visits became a regular weekly pleasure we'd have rare, but friendly, arguments.

On one occasion I dared to say, 'I can never fully understand what people see in Rembrandt. Granted he was a fine painter . . .'

'No more, please!' He held his hands high in mock horror. Then in gentle sarcasm, '"A fine painter".'

'His work is so – so – *miserable*,' I argued. 'So dark. So dismal. As if he had no real happiness in his colours.'

'At its most basic, Vincent van Gogh made us see light for the first time. Rembrandt van Rijn made us see shadows. *Shadows* . . . not merely an absence of light. Rembrandt's shadows aren't black. They don't hide things. You can see into them. See what's there. They're part of the life he recorded.'

'They're still miserable,' I insisted. 'It's their hallmark. Take his self-portrait . . .'

168

'Which one?'

'The – er . . .'

'Fifty. He painted more than fifty self-portraits.'

'Oh!'

'About the most perfect record of what the single-minded pursuit of art can do to a genius. He was married to a shrew. He was never out of debt. He drank to divorce himself from a rotten life . . . and he was honest enough to record his downward slide. From the young enthusiast to the boozed-up wreck who was denied recognition, but *knew* he was right.'

'I – er – I didn't realise . . .'

'The trouble with so many people.' For a moment he was angry. 'The name "Rembrandt". It conjures up memories of half a dozen pictures. No more. Almost seven hundred paintings – completed paintings. Three hundred etchings and another two thousand drawings. That was his output, and they're scattered all over the world. America, Russia, the United Kingdom, Spain . . . all over the world. My God, man, you're talking about a giant and you're having the impudence to criticise him because you don't understand him.'

But by this time we *could* argue. Our friendship was such that we could contradict each other, deliberately play devil's advocate sometimes, and know the bond would not slacken. It was a game, and it made living worth while.

Sal accepted him, and the three of us would walk the countryside until he'd found some view which caught his fancy, then he'd set up his easel, or take out his sketch pad and, while Sal and I continued our walk, he'd work. We'd pick him up on our way back. Wait for him to finish whatever he was doing. Then we'd stroll back to the cottage for a meal and talk and music.

He often stayed overnight. I bought a studio couch and he'd bed down there and be happy to continue our companionship at breakfast and through the following day.

169

To him I was David Deverell, a man whose past he was not interested in. I think (I *hope*) I helped him through a particularly rough period of his life. Despite everything, and even though he rarely mentioned her, I knew he missed his wife. Missed her friendship. Missed her company. At first I think I was a stop-gap, but in time I became far more.

'80, '81, '82. They were wonderful years. Peaceful and complete. I could fill these notebooks with incidents which of themselves might mean little but which, in sum, added up to everything a man like myself could wish for.

The money? It was banked, it was invested, some of it was spent. I lacked for nothing. I paid my bills within days of their arrival. Gradually I created my new self until it was complete, whole and fully documented. I filled my bookshelves. I added to my record collection. I was supremely happy.

We saw 1983 in together at the cottage. The start of another year. Another year of priceless friendship. We toasted each other in whisky, then toasted each other again and again. As the small hours crept by we grew a little tipsy. Not too much – we weren't blind drunk, or anything approaching that stage – but we were, perhaps, a little more talkative than usual, and neither of us felt like bed.

'I'm surprised,' he said.

'What at?'

'A nice chap like you. A young chap like you.'

'You're not a bad sort yourself.'

'No wife. Not even a girl-friend. Or have you?'

'Me?' I grinned a little stupidly.

'A sly dog.' He returned the grin. 'A lady on the side when I'm not here.'

'I'll have you know, I'm still a virgin.' I drew myself up in boozey pride as I made the claim.

'Now, there's a thing.' He chuckled quietly. 'You're unique, old son. In this day and age. That must be a record . . . surely?'

170

'Nothing to it.' I flopped into an armchair. 'Just don't want 'em. That's all.'

'David, my boy . . .' He lowered himself more slowly into the opposite armchair, sipped whisky, and in a more serious note said. 'They're necessary, old son. A good wife. Very necessary.'

'You should know.' I matched tone for tone.

'I *do* know. God rest her soul . . . she *was* a good wife.'

There were a few minutes of silence, then I said, 'But not easy to find.'

'What?'

'A good wife. You could end up with a bad wife.'

'Slowly.' He waved a finger, as if in warning, then continued with advice. 'You fall in love. That's the first thing. Fall in love. Make sure it's the real thing. Not a flirtation. Nothing like that. A good woman. You can *recognise* a good woman.'

'Of course.'

'Not by her looks. Dammit, there's enough good-looking bitches around. The quicksands are there, if you don't step carefully.'

'Oh, sure.'

'But a *good* woman. Keep your wits about you. You'll know. The way she reacts to certain situations. You'll know.'

'And then you fall in love,' I smiled.

'Gently. Gently.' His mind was in the past as he spoke. 'You with her. She with you. Nothing hurried. You've all life ahead of you. It comes gradually, David. Gradually and very beautifully. It's – sort of – taken for granted.'

'That you're in love with each other?'

'That. And that you're going to get married. You both know before the question's popped. That's just a formality. You can't live without each other.'

'Love,' I murmured.

'I hope it comes to you, David.' The way he said it, I suddenly realised the depth of his friendship. 'If it doesn't . . .'

He left the sentence unfinished.

Very gently, I said, 'It already has.'

171

He raised his eyebrows.

'Not marriage,' I sighed. 'That was impossible.'

'Already married?'

'No . . . other things.'

'Are there any "other things" that can't be overcome?'

'Oh, yes.' I nodded, sadly, and the past came back with a rush. 'Things you wouldn't do. Things you *couldn't* do.' I paused, then continued, 'Elizabeth. She didn't see this leg of mine. This deformity. She didn't *see* it. Only that to be completely happy we had to be together. The music, the talk . . . a little like us two. That's all she wanted. That's all *I* wanted. Lonely people. Shy people. But we weren't when we were together.'

'I'm sorry,' he murmured.

'It's why I came here. One of the reasons.'

'Do you have a photograph?'

'Just one. From a newspaper . . . that's all. I tore the page out.'

'May I?'

I went to the desk, opened a drawer and took out the page. I unfolded it and handed it to him.

'Nice.' He stared at the photograph as I returned to my chair. 'She *looks* nice, David. It comes through.' He glanced at the top of the page. 'You've kept it a long time.'

'It's all I've got.'

'And you couldn't tell her?'

'Oh, yes. I told her. It made no difference. It *couldn't* make a difference.'

'Does she visit?'

'What?' I stared.

'Here. Does she visit you?'

'My God, no! She mustn't even *know*.'

'Pity.' He carefully re-folded the page and handed it back to me. As I returned it to the desk, he said, 'You're crippled, old son. Not just the foot. Not just the back. Like me, emotionally crippled. Those who don't know . . .'

172

Again he left the sentence unfinished.

Back at the armchair I raised my glass and, with some bitterness, said, 'Here's to the emotionally crippled. Here's to their bloody misery, and the few lucky enough to be able to share it.'

'I'll drink to that.'

Thereafter, we gradually became more cheerful. The past slipped back into its place and we quietly drank and became a little drunker.

Thus, 1983. A strange beginning, as if to give the hint of an out-of-the-ordinary year. A year which, from its first few hours, had links with the past.

In the February, I began this narrative. Why? One reason was loneliness. I was snowed in; for two full weeks the drifts beat the tractors and the Land Rover. I read, listened to music, remembered, then thought it a good idea to record those memories. The good and the bad . . . they just about balanced themselves out. It wasn't meant to be a book. Just a tabulating of events. A putting in order. A record of who I *really* was . . . in case anybody ever wanted to know.

Nor did I write every day. I started in the February, made a good start, then put it aside when the snow melted. I've added to it since. Bits and pieces as I recalled them. The idea was to be as accurate as possible and as chronological as my memory would allow.

That's how it started – *when* it started – and now it has to be finished.

My schoolmaster friend got through to me on Saturday, March the 5th. He walked from the tarmac road, and it was good to see him. I made him comfortable by the fire, brewed tea and as I sat down he handed me a flat parcel.

'One of the boys,' he said as I removed the brown paper. 'His father works for *The Yorkshire Post*. It's a copy of the one they have on file. The one they took the photograph from. They only

173

needed head and shoulders, of course.'

It was Elizabeth. Full length. Standing there on the lawn of the house. He'd had it framed in a simple, slim black surround, made to stand upright wherever I wished to put it. Elizabeth. Sweet, charming Elizabeth. There! Smiling at me.

As I choked for words, he said, 'I took the liberty of noting the date on the page. It helped a lot.' He cleared his throat and muttered, 'I hope you don't mind. That I've done the right thing.'

'Only you could have thought of it,' I croaked. 'A man as kind as you. A friend like . . .' I ran out of words as the pricking behind my eyes increased. I breathed, 'Thank you. Thank you so much.'

'Drink the tea, before it gets cold,' he growled. 'And don't think that's *all* you're going to give me. I'm here for the weekend. For a good old jaw . . . see what sort of cockeyed ideas you've come up with since I saw you last.'

The photograph's home was on my bedside table. I wished it 'goodnight' and 'good morning' every day without fail. Sometimes I even talked to it; said things I would not have dared to say to Elizabeth personally. It brought back memories – vivid memories – and from those memories I filled in the spaces in these notes.

Meanwhile the weather gradually improved, and weekends came and went. The three of us wandered the surrounding country. The easel was set up, the sketch pad always at hand. Sal and I climbed the hills and discovered even more secret and secluded places. It was a poor spring; wet and cold. But the Saturday evenings and the short holidays more than made up for the weather.

We talked books, we talked painting, we talked music . . . we even talked politics when the Thatcher Government was returned to power. That, or we enjoyed long, companionable silences which, in their own way, were often more communicative than all the talk in the world.

174

I still took *The Yorkshire Post*. I had arranged for it to be put to one side for me each day. Newspaper delivery was out of the question, therefore about twice a week I drove to the newsagent's and collected my copies. That all bar one was out of date wasn't important. The radio kept me abreast of what world or national news interested me. *The Yorkshire Post* merely provided good articles and opinions and, once a week, reviewed the latest books and records on the market. It gave me necessary guide-lines for my chosen way of life. Nevertheless, I usually glanced through the local news, and on Monday, July the 4th I saw the half-column news that my step-mother had died. It was news of the funeral, really. How she'd been held in great esteem and that brand of post mortem rubbish. The wreaths and who'd sent them. And the list of mourners. 'Sir Raymond Cutter' headed the list, of course, and a handful of names I'd never heard of. *But no Elizabeth.*

Elizabeth was her true daughter, you must remember. Not 'step'. Not 'half'. Her *daughter*. What was more she was Elizabeth and, despite the dreary non-personality of my step-mother, Elizabeth should have been there – *would* have been there – to pay a daughter's last respects.

At first it was merely a puzzle. Perhaps an omission on the part of the reporter covering the funeral. Perhaps a lack of column space, and inadvertently the news editor had scored out Elizabeth's name. A dozen reasons, none of them important, merely that the absence of her name tended to annoy me. It cast a slur upon her honesty and sense of duty.

I know I talked to her photograph that night before I went to sleep. I held it in my hands and said, 'They do you an injustice, my darling. They don't know you, as I know you. Of course you were there. Newspapers are notorious for that sort of thing. They don't realise the hurt they sometimes cause. You were there. I *know* you were there.'

I stared at the photograph for even longer than usual. Seeing the face. Seeing the background. Seeing the lawn and the garden, and the clumps of daffodils just starting to burst into

175

their first glory. I had strange pangs of homesickness. After all it *was* my home and my heritage. And she was the only woman who'd ever entered my life . . . or who ever would.

At last, I sighed, replaced the photograph, turned off the light and tossed in restless sleep until dawn.

The mind in sleep – even in half-sleep – takes upon itself a life of its own. It remembers things, solves problems, poses questions, and in some strange way reaches conclusions which, while it is under the control of its owner, it can never reach. The photograph, for example. It was wrong, and when I climbed from bed I knew it was wrong and knew *why* it was wrong.

Head and shoulders, you see. For some three years and more I'd accepted the head and shoulders picture in the newspaper. Then I'd been given the full-length photograph and (naturally) I had taken it for granted that the newspaper photographer had taken more than one shot and, from his work, somebody had cut down the full-length picture to head and shoulders as a means of saving space.

And I'd been wrong!

'The daffodils. Daffodils do *not* burst into flower on lawns in late November, and the photograph showed daffodils. Distinctly and easily recognisable. Fine . . . it meant (it *could* have meant) that *The Yorkshire Post* had asked for a photograph and had been given one taken earlier that year. It was possible. It was even likely. If (as the solicitor's statement had intimated) she'd gone away to escape the publicity it was *very* likely.

Nevertheless . . .

All that day I was haunted by possibilities. I tried coincidence for size, but it did little to quieten my agitation. The photograph hadn't been taken when it *should* have been taken. Her name was missing from the list of mourners at her mother's funeral. Two tiny straws. Even together they added up to very little . . . until you added Raymond and the cock-and-bull story he'd told about *my* death at the hands of non-existent kidnappers.

The next day I could contain myself no longer. By dawn I was in the Land Rover, heading for the forest. *My* forest. The forest and the air-raid shelter. The place I thought I'd never have to visit again. And yet I must be careful how I word this. To say I was suspicious would be an exaggeration. Worried, perhaps. Anxious to remove a possibility. That, and fear. A fear I wished to prove groundless.

I remembered the ground. Of course I did. It had once been *my* ground. Sal's birthplace. I still knew every track and every tree, and with the Land Rover I could penetrate the forest farther than I'd been able to do with the Polo.

I left Sal in the car and walked the last two miles. Alone and frightened. Soft-footed and with my eyes and ears alert to catch sight or sound of the unusual. Then at last I reached the gulley and slowly, hesitantly, took the last half-dozen steps.

She was there!

God help me, she was there, and I almost fainted when I saw her . . . saw what was left of her. I recognised the hair. I recognised the material of the dress. The rest? Nobody could have recognised it. Nature's scavengers had been at work. That and weather and putrefaction. The ants, the vermin and the foulness to which all flesh is heir had done their work well. The stench was bad, but it must once have been abominable. The face of the skull was soiled bone, and the empty eye-sockets showed disgusting hollowness and, still in position around the neck, was the chain. The chain which had once held him prisoner and which he'd used to strangle her, once he was free.

My Elizabeth. My love. It was like opening a grave and seeing . . .

The next thing I recall I was back at the Land Rover being violently sick.

The mad blood of the Cutter family. The *bad* blood of the Cutter family. That's what it boiled down to. That's what it will always boil down to. Father. Raymond. Myself. Oh yes, I counted myself as one of those in whom it ran. Twisted and deformed; a hermit; a man not wanting the normal world or anything that world could offer. A man prepared to use an illegal trap and fake a kidnapping, rather than trust the truth with the police. Indeed, the blood was in me, too. A little diluted, perhaps. A little more controlled. A little less wild . . . but still there.

Something about desperate diseases. Desperate remedies. Certainly desperation. Raymond had lived too long; four, five years too long. He had to go. He had to be stopped, before he married and perpetuated the line and passed on that blood.

I drove back to my cottage in the Cleveland Hills. I drove slowly, because I was trembling with a mixture of shock and rage every inch of the way. Five times I stopped at lay-bys, to weep a little and to gain control of myself. I had sense enough to know I was a menace to other motorists, but I had to get back. I had to *think*. To plan something beyond normal retribution. Something only a Cutter could think of. Something mad. Bad. Something appropriate.

It took me two days to quieten down. Two days and two nights, sitting hunched in the armchair, alternating between whisky and black coffee. The madness was there. The touch of insanity. But because of this I was able to remove myself from the horror by the Anderson shelter; to make believe that Elizabeth was still around; that the photograph on my bedside table *was* Elizabeth . . . not the other thing in the gulley.

Objectivity, you see. The brain can do it. It needs a shock – the sort of shock capable of hurling you over the edge – but if you can withstand that shock, if you can fight it and beat it, imprison it in a straitjacket up there in your skull, you end up with objectivity. The objectivity of the surgeon's knife. The objectivity that can do anything. Anything! Thereafter, there was no problem. Even time didn't matter. I had all the time in the world. The plan had been worked out. The machine had been created. It would work . . . when *I* wanted it to work. Not

178

Raymond. Raymond had no say in the matter. Raymond was nothing. In effect, he was already dying and praying for a quick end. That he didn't yet *know* was neither here nor there. *I* set the time. *I* set the tempo. It was already out of Raymond's hands.

On the Thursday, I drove to Scarborough, sought out a solicitor and made my will. The will of David Deverell. All my goods, all my property, all my cash and shares. Everything to the last penny . . . to the only friend I had.

He'd be surprised, but he deserved it. He'd shown me the truth. The photograph . . . without that I would have never known.

And it *was* my money. From the first, that half million had been *mine*. I hadn't stolen it. I hadn't fleeced anybody. Indeed, in my true identity I was worth far more than a paltry half million. Far more. But I didn't *want* my true identity. I wasn't a 'Cutter' any more. I was David Deverell; a mild eccentric who lived alone and paid his debts.

Solicitors don't like to be hurried and this one was no exception. He hummed and hawed, but I insisted. Dammit, it wasn't a complicated will. Everything to one man. No qualifications. The lot . . . *his*. So (and, I suspect, against his every natural instinct) the solicitor agreed, had the will drawn up, had my signature witnessed, then kept the original and gave me a photostat copy.

It can be done, you see. Merely press. Merely demand. Impose your will upon these small, insignificant people. They buckle. *You* hold the reins and the whip – you are employing *them*, not the other way round – and, with a little pressure, they buckle.

That last weekend together was something of an ordeal. I suppose it showed on my face. In the spurt and stop of my conversation. I tried, and almost succeeded, but I couldn't *quite* act normally. Naturally. I was uneasy and I couldn't hide it.

'Something wrong?' he asked. 'Off colour?'

'No.'

'You don't look too good.'

'I'm fine.'

'You don't look "fine". You look as if you're worried about something.'

'Worried? What the hell have *I* to worry about?'

He moved his shoulders and didn't press the matter, but I caught him glancing at me when he thought I wasn't watching. *He* was worried . . . but I wasn't. What had I to worry about? I was in the driving seat, and I had control. Both speed and direction were mine to decide. I loved the man – of course I loved the man – I loved him like a son loves a father. Not *my* father. A *real* father. That's how much I loved him. But I didn't need advice. From anybody!

As he left on the Sunday evening, he said, 'See a doctor, David.'

'Why?'

'There's something wrong with you, old son.'

'Wrong?'

'Your nerves. Maybe living here alone.'

'I have Sal.'

'Sal's only a dog,' he pleaded. 'She can only help so much.'

'I don't need help.'

'I think you do.' There was sombre concern in the statement.

'I'll see a doctor,' I promised.

'Good. When?'

'Before I see you next.'

'Good.' He smiled and the handshake was a little tighter –a little longer – than usual. 'That's a promise, remember. See a doctor before you see me next.'

When he'd gone, I laughed quietly. A joke, you see. 'Before I saw him next'. Oh, yes, I'd see a doctor. As I understood things, it would be a very special kind of doctor . . . and *he'd* see *me*.

I'd kept the Smith and Wesson oiled and in working order. Why? I can't give a satisfactory answer. Not really. Why *do* men keep firearms, look at them, handle them, keep them clean and in good working order? The shrinks might spout theories about phallic symbolism. Crap, of course. What the hell do *they* know about madness? They've never been mad. Only the mad know about madness; its countless degrees; its beautiful inverted sanity. Don't believe the shrinks. They invent big words for simple things. The truth? Sanity is madness, and madness is sanity carried to its ultimate conclusion. Madness? The worm of truth which eventually eats away falsehood and leaves only sanity. Pure, burning, blazing sanity, but the shrinks call it madness. They grow rich, and fat, and shiny on a confidence trick.

I oiled and cleaned the revolver that night. I oiled and cleaned the five bullets left in its chambers. I dry-fired it a score of times. It would work. Oh yes, come the moment, it would work.

I re-loaded the gun, then put it to one side and talked to Sal.

I told her what I was going to do. Explained everything in detail . . . in order that she might understand and forgive. I told her I loved her, but that she had no part in this thing I had to do. This was a solo run (I explained) and therefore I must leave her for some hours. That she mustn't worry. That it was my decision, not hers. That, whatever happened to me, she'd be taken care of. I assured her upon that point and she understood. As always . . . she understood everything. Perfectly.

By dawn, this morning (Monday, July 11th) I was on the outskirts of my forest. Not yet inside the forest, but at an isolated telephone kiosk within easy walking distance of where I planned to be. I'd parked the Land Rover half a mile away, in a little-used lay-by. It was safe. It would be there when I needed it. When what had to be done had *been* done. I

181

had a row of 10p pieces ready before I dialled the number of the house.

It took all of five minutes before anybody answered and, from the sleepy slur of the voice, it was obvious that the man had just climbed from his bed.

I hung a folded handkerchief over the mouthpiece and said, 'I wish to speak to Sir Raymond Cutter.'

'Who is that?'

'A man who wishes to speak to Sir Raymond Cutter.'

'I'm afraid I . . .'

'Don't argue,' I snapped.

'. . . he's still in bed.'

'Get him out of bed.'

'If you can give me your name and the nature of your business.'

'I'll give you some advice,' I said in a hard, flat tone. 'If I have to ring a second time, I'll tell him of this call . . . and you'll be looking for another job. That much, I promise.'

'If . . .' He cleared his throat. 'If you'll give me *some* indication.'

'Tell him I've recently seen his sister.'

'I don't think . . .'

'Just that!' My patience was growing short. 'Just that message. Tell him it *now*. And that I'm waiting at this end to hear from him.'

It took less than five minutes. I fed 10p pieces into the slot until Raymond's voice came over the wire.

'Who the hell's . . .'

'Quieten down!' I interrupted. 'I've seen your sister. I thought you'd like to know.'

'Who is that?' His voice had a choking quality.

'We'll come to that later. Eventually.' I chuckled. 'Meanwhile, I think we should meet.'

'Meet?' He was really off-balance. I could visualise him, ashen-faced and panic-stricken. The mental picture amused me. Pleased me.

'The three of us,' I amplified.

'The – the . . .'

'You, me and Elizabeth.' I paused, then added, 'As you know, she can't travel easily.'

'Look! What the . . .'

'Three o'clock, this afternoon. I think I can get there in time. I know *you* can.'

'What – what do you want?' he breathed.

'Whatever you have to offer. We'll discuss the details at three o'clock. Be there . . . otherwise I might send for somebody else.'

I dropped the receiver onto its rest, stuffed the handkerchief into my pocket and left the kiosk. I hurried into the forest, along paths and short-cuts only I knew. I tried to imagine what he was doing. Out of bed. A bath? Perhaps a bath, perhaps a shower, perhaps just a quick wash. A shave? No . . . I didn't think he'd stop for a shave. Breakfast, perhaps? I thought not. At the most a snack; possibly a cup of coffee. If not coffee, a stiff drink. He'd *need* a stiff drink. Then he'd dress. Dress hurriedly. Three o'clock be damned. He'd want to be there long before three o'clock. He'd want to be there *first*.

On the other hand, he might take time to quieten down. To steady his nerves. That 'I think I can get there' remark I'd made had been meant to give me the edge as far as time was concerned. If he'd swallowed the bait he might not be in such a big hurry. First, of course. He'd certainly want to be there first. But if he'd believed me, 'first' meant some time before three o'clock.

I couldn't risk it, though. I couldn't risk *anything*. This was the last move in a game we'd been playing for years. I had to win it . . . it, and the game. The game ended today. Finished! No more moves. No more anything.

I came to the holly bush; the holly bush I pointed out to Elizabeth so long ago. I approached it from the left fork, then turned back on myself by taking the right fork. The way he'd come. The way he *had* to come short of carrying a machete with

183

which to slash a way through the undergrowth. Past the silver birch and the short-nibbled grass; glimpsing the powder-puff tail of the last rabbit to scamper into hiding at my approach. The double-bend and the ancient oak.

That was my chosen rendezvous. The oak, and its great gnarled bole, and its 'court' of lesser, younger trees scattered around the exposed roots. Roots like twisted, arthritic fingers trying to force themselves into a fist. Where I'd meet him. Where, for the first time, he'd *know*.

I chuckled quietly at the prospect. He wouldn't hear me. I wore rope-soled sandals and clothes which didn't 'squeak' or rustle. Like a ghost. Dammit I *was* a ghost. I was dead. On his own evidence, I was dead. Blown to a bloody eternity by his kidnappers, years ago. I didn't exist. The sweet, pure logic of it all. He was keeping an appointment with a dead man, because of a dead woman. It was all catching up on him. Pay-day had arrived.

I chose my hiding place. I'd hear him, I'd see him, before he saw me. Of course I would. This was still *my* forest. I'd hear him, see him and, when he was aware of my presence, it would be too late. I took out the Smith and Wesson, checked it, thumbed off the safety catch, then settled down with my back against a tree. I placed the revolver in my lap and waited. I could wait. If necessary, I could wait forever.

It was 10.22 a.m. when I first heard him. That is the exact time. I glanced at my watch. It was 10.22 a.m. I could hear him fifty yards before he came into sight. He made no attempt at a silent approach. He was so damn sure. He'd accepted the three o'clock remark at face value, and he was going to be there *well* before three o'clock. He was safe. He was Raymond – Sir Raymond Cutter, Bt. – and nobody could pull the wool over *his* eyes. He was going to be there *first* . . . well before three o'clock.

I pushed myself gently to my feet, thumbed the hammer of the Smith and Wesson and put the firing pin in its hair-trigger position. One little touch. Pressure hardly heavy enough to break a spider's web . . . and that would be my visiting card. I grinned happily at the thought.

I stood, motionless, as he passed. He didn't see me. He *couldn't* see me. He didn't know the trick. Silent and still, alongside the trunk of a tree and half-hidden by a thin curtain of foliage. He could have passed and re-passed a dozen times, he still wouldn't have seen me. He had a twin-barrelled twelve-bore tucked under his right arm. He was ready for anything. Or thought he was. Cunning . . . but clumsy. He caught a foot on one of the exposed roots. *My* forest, you see. *My* territory. He hadn't a chance.

I moved up behind him, raised the revolver and sent the first round through his right shoulder blade. It spun him slightly, threw him forward and onto the ground and the twelve-bore slipped and clattered onto the oak's roots.

As I stooped to pick up the shot-gun he yelled with pain, clutched his smashed shoulder and twisted to look up at me.

'Good morning, Raymond,' I said politely.

'Who the hell . . .'

'I was – what is it? . . . aiming at a wood-pigeon.'

'Who the . . .' For a moment the beard put him off, then he recognised me. His teeth tightened against the pain and he snarled, 'It's you, you bastard. It was *you* who telephoned this . . .'

'I'm not here,' I reminded him. 'I'm dead . . . remember? How can a dead man use a telephone?'

He remained silent. Glaring his hatred. The blood running through the fingers which clutched his right shoulder.

I dropped the revolver into my pocket and cocked both hammers of the twelve-bore.

'On your feet, little brother,' I ordered.

'I'm damned if . . .'

'I can see another wood-pigeon,' I smiled. 'To your left this time. I'm a lousy shot. I might miss it.'

He climbed to his feet. Slowly. Painfully. I prodded him with the twelve-bore.

185

'Let's keep the appointment.'

'What?'

'With Elizabeth. We're a little early, but she won't mind. She's already there.'

'Look, I don't know what . . .'

'You're going,' I assured him. 'Your only choice is *how* you go. You can walk. Or I can knock the other arm out of action and drag you . . . feet first. That's your choice. Don't waste time. Make it.'

'You wouldn't. You . . .'

I think his mouth dried on him. I think he realised, for the first time, that whatever *he* was, *I* was . . . plus. This was no 'Anderson Shelter' game of hide-and-seek; bluff and counter-bluff; kidology, to keep him off my back for a while. He was within a trigger-squeeze of having his flesh torn from his body and the choice was his, because I didn't give a damn either way.

He turned and walked ahead of me. Stumbling a little. Bow shouldered. Gripping his injured shoulder with his left hand. He walked as slowly as he dared, but that was all right by me. He was prolonging his own fear and his own pain, and that pleased me. Neither of us spoke.

He paused as he reached the gulley. He turned and tears crept down his cheeks.

'If you're going to kill me, kill me,' he pleaded.

'I'm not going to kill you, little brother.' My voice was flat and hard. I felt no pity for him. He'd felt no pity for *her*.

'I – I don't want to see,' he whispered.

'Get down that bank,' I rasped. 'Get down. *See* her.'

'Please.'

'*See her.*' I rammed the muzzles into his side. 'See her . . . or I'll throw you down on top of her.'

Reluctantly – slowly – he inched his way down the bank and into the gulley. He kept his head sideways, his eyes averted, frightened to even look.

'Back against the birch,' I ordered and he obeyed, but still he couldn't look at the thing I'd once loved.

186

I dropped down and stood by the door of the shelter. The foulness that had been Elizabeth lay stretched between us.

'Like old times,' I observed with a smile.

'Lionel, for God's sake . . .'

'Who's "Lionel"? "Lionel" has been dead years. Right? He died, rescuing you from kidnappers. I'm not "Lionel". I'm the man who's *not* going to kill you.'

I squeezed one of the triggers, and his left shoulder was torn to bloody ribbons. The force of the shot buffeted him against the birch, then he slipped down into a faint.

I leaned the shotgun against the wall of the shelter, then took the key to the second padlock from my pocket and unlocked the chain from its concrete anchor. With infinite care – loving care – I raised the skull and unwound the chain from the neck. I felt no repugnance. This was Elizabeth. *My* Elizabeth. She was beautiful; far too beautiful for putrefaction to mask that beauty.

I wound the chain around my hand then dropped it onto the bench in the shelter . . . then waited.

He groaned quietly before he came out of his faint, then gradually became conscious. He couldn't speak. I don't think he could bring himself to unlock his jaw. He was in pain. Great pain. But alive. He sprawled with his head against the birch, blood running from both shoulders and his legs stretched straight in front of him.

I took the revolver from my pocket and walked over. His eyes widened in terror.

'I'm not going to kill you,' I soothed. 'I made a promise. I keep my promises. Not to kill you. A little pain, perhaps. It's known as knee-capping.'

I thumbed back the hammer, lowered the muzzle and, from less than eighteen inches, blew his left knee-cap off. He screamed. High, tight and loud. He made an involuntary attempt to grasp the shattered knee but the movement brought pain to his shoulders and the scream tailed off into a shuddering moan. This time he didn't faint. I think pain can be

187

great enough to counter-balance the blessing of unconsciousness. He just stared. Terrified. Wondering what was coming next.

I gave him time enough to grow used to the increased agony. It seemed right. Right that he should suffer a little. A lesson, perhaps. A demonstration that he was not the only one. That other people could be a little thoughtless – a little selfish – when necessary. I walked over to the shelter, picked up the twelve-bore and fired the remaining shot into the trees. Then I broke the gun and the two spent cartridges flipped out and fell to the ground.

'I don't need this,' I smiled. 'Nor do you.'

I flung the shot-gun high and away beyond the rear of the shelter.

I took the Smith and Wesson and returned to where he was sprawling. I thumbed back the trigger and took careful aim. I smiled down at him. I even felt pity. Not compassion, you understand. Pity. Pity that his life had been so evil; that this was necessary in order to even things out. He shouldn't have done all those things, you see. It amazed and saddened me that he seemed to misunderstand. *I* wasn't enjoying this. It was just something that had to be done and, unfortunately, I was the only person able to do it. To show him the error of his ways. To make him a better man.

I touched the trigger and the knee-cap of his right leg shattered. His whole body jerked, his eyes rolled until only the whites showed then, slowly, he regained some sort of control over himself.

'I'm not going to kill you,' I assured him.

He moved his head in a jerking, nodding movement. Pleading. Asking me to break my word. It angered me.

'I don't kill people,' I snapped. 'Damnation, what sort of man do you think I am?' Then my anger evaporated, and I smiled. 'You're all right, little brother. You might not walk again. Your arms might be useless. These are possibilities. But you still have a trunk. You still have a head. You're not dead, boy. You'll live . . . if you're found.' I moved to Elizabeth, bent and lifted the neckline of the rotting cloth. I thrust the revolver deep into the mush that had once been her body. Cold mush, that moved and wriggled across my skin. I straightened, then bent again to wipe my hand on the skirt of Raymond's jacket. Then I stood up, and pointed. 'It's there,' I explained. 'Two rounds left. If you feel the need to use them – on yourself – all you have to do is take it. Elizabeth won't mind. You've made sure she won't mind. Just *get* there. That's your problem. No legs, no arms. Quite a problem . . . but *yours*.'

I collected the chain, dropped it into my pocket, and left.

Not unreasonable, I think. Not *too* unreasonable. Melodramatic, perhaps. Perhaps? But appropriate. I cannot be convinced that it was other than appropriate.

I sit here, writing the last of these notes, and have no regrets. No regrets, and not much time. Perhaps time enough for explanations . . . if explanations are really necessary.

I think we all live lies. I think none of us dare face the unadorned truth. That, for example, *I* killed my father. Indirectly, of course, but with no less certainty. The fake kidnapping brought to light the Smith and Wesson; introduced Rucker into the scheme of things; resulted in Father being arrested. Go back far enough . . . *I* killed him. At the very least I was responsible for his death. That, for example, *I* killed Elizabeth. I sent her the letter, I sent her the key. I showed her the way through my forest. The actual strangulation was performed by Raymond . . . but *I* was the one who sent her, and *I* was the one who chained Raymond and provided the murder weapon. Again, without me, she would not be dead. My step-mother? Who knows? The death of my father, the tragedy upon tragedy. I don't know the cause of her death, but my own actions can only have hastened that death.

On my way back – shortly before I reached home – I telephoned the local police station. I asked that they visit here at half-past eight. As punctual as possible. Something very

189

urgent. They were curious. Therefore they will come. It is now almost eight o'clock.

I count myself a fairly lucky man. For what I am, a *very* lucky man. I have never known want nor yearned for luxury. I have known the love of one fine woman and equally the love of one fine man. For me that is sufficient. That and my dog. I have deserved none of it. My nature, my personality, has been my main enemy. Loners are people carrying their own curse around with them. Introverts in a world of extroverts. I have tried, so hard, to remain sane. Tried. Sometimes with success . . . sometimes without. I am certainly sane at this moment, as I pen the final sentences to a story which had to be told.

The chain is already looped over the beam in the bedroom. The table is in position. The noose will be completed with the help of the padlock, and the key will be well beyond my reach. The weapon that killed her will kill me. I confess to a certain desire for it to be quick. I am told that if the knot is placed under the left jaw-bone, and if the drop is long enough, the knot is jerked forward, under the chin, and the neck is broken. I am hopeful that the padlock will do the same.

These are not morbid thoughts. I am weary of the deception. The make-believe that I am not, at times, insane; that the Cutter blood does not flow through *my* veins, too. I have (and I admit it) lived a life of complete non-achievement. A selfish life, with no purpose and nothing to show for it. In that, I am no better than all the other Cutters. Father, Raymond, Step-mother, even Elizabeth. We have earned nothing. Not even respect.

The will? I wish it to be understood that, although it was made out as from and signed by 'David Deverell' I insist that its terms be followed. That things proceed as if 'David Deverell' *had* made the will. I leave these instructions as the present Sir Lionel Cutter, Baronet. I insist they be followed.

And now time runs short. I shall place this manuscript in an envelope marked 'Urgent' on the bed near my hanging body. I shall leave a copy of the will alongside it.

But before I go . . .

I know Raymond. Know him better than any other man alive. I made him a promise. That I would not kill him. He is injured – badly injured – but despite the pain he will hang onto life. I doubt if he will worm his way to the body of Elizabeth. I doubt if he will be able to. I am certain he will not be able to reach for the Smith and Wesson. He will still be alive. Instructions for reaching him are in these notes.

A lesson, you see. A stern lesson. A lesson even *he* will never forget . . . plus the fact that he is alongside what is left of the woman he murdered. He has *that* to pay for too.

How to end?

Quickly and simply. With all the other Cutters, I'll see you in Hell.